T0117284

EQUITY 5

SEPP ETTERER

Order this book online at www.trafford.com
or email orders@trafford.com

Most Trafford titles are also available at major online book retailers.

© Copyright 2012 Sepp Etterer.
All rights reserved. No part of this publication may be reproduced, stored in a retrieval
system, or transmitted, in any form or by any means, electronic, mechanical, photocopying,
recording, or otherwise, without the written prior permission of the author.

Printed in the United States of America.

ISBN: 978-1-4669-4181-6 (sc)
ISBN: 978-1-4669-4840-2 (e)

Trafford rev. 07/11/2012

 www.trafford.com

North America & international
toll-free: 1 888 232 4444 (USA & Canada)
phone: 250 383 6864 ♦ fax: 812 355 4082

Dedication

I dedicate this book to my wife, Judith, who helped bring me back from the dark side, who works harder than I and doesn't believe in free lunch.

FOREWORD

T HE IDEA FOR this book struck me in 1976 while I was working as the senior safety manager at a three unit fossil fuel power plant in the Navaho Nation near Page, Arizona. That's a whole other story equally as absurd. Anyway I was living in a trailer with not much to do. Can you believe I got a $200 ticket for too much tumbleweed on my non-existing lawn that I didn't put there? I enjoyed an occasional chess game at the Wahweap Lodge. I even got to chat with Richard Burton one night. He noticed I was smoking a calabash pipe and inquired about it. Back to the book—my electrical engineering training did not really prepare me to write a book and this was my third attempt (don't bother to look for them). What was different about writing this book was that I didn't really write it. I held the pencil but it just sort of took over and wrote itself. It was downright exciting. I felt like I was reading it as it appeared on the page.

You are probably wondering how I went from herding cows in Bavaria to flying jets in America to wearing a bullet proof vest in Bessemer, Alabama but that's another story. I can say that God—whom I denied for many decades—decided I needed extra time to get my act together because I'm a slow learner.

I hope you enjoy this book and that it makes you mad and remember there is no free lunch.

CHAPTER 1

GREEN BAY WAS a better than average mid-west community. Belgian names took up most of the pages in the phone book. Paper manufacture surrounded by agriculture groomed a working class with little unemployment or crime. The fine arts were represented by local theaters, many artists and a decent symphony orchestra. Football and high per capita beer consumption blended with two academic institutions of liberal gestations. Most restaurants had red decor, abounding in vinyl and felt flock wall paper. The wine lists often consisted of red, white and pink. Bowling alleys were usually overbooked with company teams and loud, overweight women.

The Gourmet House was different. This establishment was owned and operated by Richard Greenwood. Greenwood was originally from San Fransisco where he made an impressive fortune as a construction worker. Years of overtime, dilligent work and frugal living were accumulated for the downpayment of an ailing restaurant on the west side of Green Bay. This was his dream: To operate a classy restaurant away from the heavy competition of San Fransisco.

Greenwood immediately opened a small section of the place while he rebuilt the rest. Everything became a feast for eyes: The patterned, hard wood floors, chandeliers, plants, table settings, menu and especially the waitresses. The clientel showed their appreciation by keeping the tables full and paying the lofty tabs. The owner himself was nothing like his restaurant—except perhaps the foundation. He dressed and spoke like a common worker. He was uncomplimentary but impeccably honest. Few of his patrons knew him nor would have wanted to. Although he had a very capable assistant, Greenwood insisted on personally approving the ingredients of recipies, counting receivables and hiring all waitresses.

One of the ladies who came out from San Fransisco to work for him had to return on short notice. Greenwood was interviewing for a replacement. "OK. Thanks a lot for coming in, Miss . . . ah . . ."

"Trevon."

"Right. Listen, we'll give you a call if we need you."

"Thank you, Mr. Greenwood. Good bye."

"Good bye, now . . . Hey, Howard! Come here for a minute?"

"Be right in, Dick," said a muffled voice from a nearby storeroom.

"Hey, you know those five women you lined up for me?"

"Yea."

"Dogs. You got me a goddamn truckload a' DOGS!"

"I didn't line them up. Just put an ad in the paper is all. How's I s'posed to know what they looked like?"

"Still dogs. Did you see them?"

"Well, I couldn't miss one of them. Looks like she eats most of her orders before she delivers 'em."

"Goddamn right. Dogs everyone of them. One had acne so bad I was scared to ask her anything 'n case she shook her head to answer."

Howard began to grin but saw Greenwood's anger flare: "The last one had dents for boobs and this Flosy—Flossy broad. Jesus. Like a Halloween pumpkin. Do you think people wonna be waited on by teeth like that? . . . Huh?"

Greenwood demanded from no one in particular.

"Look, I'm sorry . . ."

And sorry they would be for leaving the office window open. It was this window that anyone leaving the Gourmet House would have to pass enroute to the parking lot. And it was Miss Alice Trevon who overheard the shouting, including the reference to her lack of prominent breasts. Her face flushed with indignation. She made it to her car in disciplined silence. When she had slammed the door, the sound from her throat was a high pitched wretch powered by a store of anger and pain. Alice

Trevon kept mostly to herself. At the age of twenty-seven she had had few second dates and certainly no hint of marriage. "That disgusting pig," she hissed into the purse groping for a pencil. She was fed up with missing the good things in life for something as unimportant as small breasts. Her confidence, which would otherwise have been sparkling, was always dimmed by this deficiency. Now she tried remembering the names of the other four women waiting with her in the Gourmet House lobby. "Those inconsiderate jerks invited all five to show up at the same time," she fumed. Then Alice made a plan to right this wrong.

*   *   *

A plume of cigar smoke came out of Greenwood's office, followed by: "Howard!"

Howard had almost escaped to the men's room but felt unable to ignore the call. Greenwood always waited until he was down the hall before calling him back. It was an obsession like turning on a light to see if it was still working. "Coming," came from clenched teeth.

"Howie," this familiarity announcing an imposition, "I want somebody—tonight! Otherwise we might get stuck without enough help again. No more newspaper shit. You find somebody and stay out of the damned kennels.

And if she ain't got big tits and a dairy queen smile, don't bring her. In fact don't come back until you got one.

Think you can handle that?" Greenwood's eyes dropped back to his paperwork and dismissed Howard, who left without reply.

The newspaper ad was bought at Greenwood's request. Sometimes, Howard thought, his own main function was to absorb the fruits of Greenwood's errors and act as a general buffer between him and the employees. Although it had been a trying eight months, he certainly had learned from Greenwood how to make a restaurant go. The place had real class. It became so popular that Greenwood was planning to open another by the end of the year. Greenwood knew what class was, although he did not allow the concept to phase his own behavior. So, the future hinted at many reasons for Howard to stand by in this hour of need while trying to ignore the abuse.

Howard began mentally turning the pages of his address book, searching for a new employee. It was good his own job did not depend on looks because he did not seem able to attract any women that would fit Greenwood's parameters. Suddenly, a vision of a smiling queen with huge mammaries drifted across his fantasy and transposed itself into the likeness of Lil. Howard's mind now reeled at the possibilities. Lil was a student until two weeks ago when lack of funds brought enlightenment to a standstill. He had overheard the description of her plight to a drooling admirer named something-or-other Cranston. Lil Sanchez. Normally, she would not look twice at him, he concluded. Once her full name came fully into grasp, Howard pushed the brake pedal into the phonebooth just ahead. The driver of a Porshe tooted and gave him the finger which Howard accepted without response. He found the S's and to his joy zeroed in on Sanchez, L. Single women usually listed only their first initial so no one would know they were single. Or women. The first quarter fell, richocheted off his trouser and passed through the vent louvre. He produced another and inserted it carefully with symptoms of palsy nearly again propelling the coin to the ground. 'You gotta be home,' he thought. Four rings. Maybe she is taking a bath. Howard fantasized Lil wrapping a towel around her glistening body to answer the phone when she did indeed answer the phone.

"Hello."

"Hi. Can I talk to Lil, please," he heard himself utter—thankful the answering party could not witness his condition.

"Who is this, please?"

"Oh, this is Howard," realizing this would fail to impress, "the bartender at the Gourmet House."

"The guy with the glasses and sort of blonde hair, right?"

Howard did not know if this was a double insult or demonstration of superb memory. "Hey, good mam—ah memory. How are you?"

"Freezing actually. I just got out of the tub."

'Christ,' Howard thought and hoped he had not said it.

"Oh, I'm sorry. I'll make it quick. You kind of impressed me the other night . . ."

And just as Howard examined his importance in this matter, Lil extinguished his mood with: "Wait—I can save you a lot of time and anxiety by telling you I'm going with a guy. In fact, the one you saw me with."

To cover his crash, he continued in a more formal: "Oh, please. That's not why I called. This is purely business."

"Oh—yea? What kind of?"

"I overheard that you were seeking employment and as we suddenly found ourselves needing an additional waitress, I thought of you."

"Well . . . alright. I'm listening."

"Good," he said this as if she were passing an oral exam, "as you probably know, we cater to the, shall we say, more sophisticated members of our community and therefore need to be represented by waitresses who appear equally as sophisticated." He was quite proud of this delivery and knew she would be able to extract the intended compliments.

Instead: "O.K., cut the bullshit. You like my body and my face and you want me to work for you, right?"

"In a manner of speaking, yes."

"In a manner of speaking, how much do you pay?"

That had not been discussed with Greenwood but Howard had a good idea of the intended range: "Seven and a half an hour plus tips. You keep your own."

"You know, the fix I'm in, I just might take you up on that."

"I certainly hope so."

"When would you want me to start?"

"Tonight. At five."

"You guys really plan ahead. What did you say your name was again?"

"Howard. Howard Atkinson. But Howie will do," he added, giving her that much.

"This is a bit sudden but I'll see you at five . . . Oh, what do I wear?"

"Just wear a nice, low cut dress tonight and we'll get you fixed up with a uniform later."

"O.K. You're not expecting any fringe benefits, are you?"

"Certainly not," Howard protested, "this is purely business."

"O.K. See you, boss."

This final confirmation of his authority, apparently lacking in mockery, allowed him to return to the office and non-chelantly describe his acquisition as if he could produce ten more on a moments notice.

* * *

"Hello. R-R-Ryan resid-d-dence."

"Hello. Can I speak with Gwen Ryan please." This was Alice Trevon, perched at her telephone. Still angry and ready for business.

"This is she."

"My name is Alice Trevon and I'm one of the women that applied for the Gourmet House job today. I sat next to you in the lobby?"

"Oh, h-h-hi! Say, I s-s-sure hope I can I-I-land that job. It's a lovely place a-a-and they p-p-pay six dollars a-a- an hour. Oh, but I g-g-guess you're hoping as h-h-hard as I am."

"No, not really and I'll tell you why." Which she did and then several more times. Alice felt awkward using the word 'dogs' while she was inciting to riot. It was all set up then. Tomorrow night everyone would meet at Alice's apartment, talk a bit and later move on to dine at the Gourmet House.

Alice was proud of the way she had decorated her apartment and welcomed the opportunity to show it off. It had some nice furnishings but mainly reflected a peaceful, creative person. The paintings were mostly her own. A few dreamy posters suggested the quest for utopia. Most of the plants were from donated slips—sometimes referred to as 'her babies' with some being anything but. An adequate bookshelf was offset by a high shool vintage bust of Mozart. No one could correctly say she was a radical. She worked in the County Clerk's office in an isolated room. Actually, this is what drove Alice to answer the advertisement. She did not need the money although six dollars plus tips was good for such work. Mainly, she just wanted to be around nice, refined people that might appreciate her personality. Some place like the Gourmet House. No one could have appreciated the determination it required for her to answer the help wanted ad. The last thing she wanted or expected was to be called a flat chested dog.

The door chime announced the first guest. A smartly dressed woman confidently introduced herself to Alice: "Hi, I'm Jennifer Lockhardt."

"Come on in. I'm glad you could make it." Immediately Alice felt intimidated. Jennifer walked in, placed her purse on a coffee table and sat down as if she held part ownership. Alice offered coffee. Jennifer declined.

During an awkward period of silence, Jennifer waited to be entertained. Alice already was having second thoughts about pursuing the cause. Jennifer thought about an Amway presentation she was once coerced into. She looked around and saw no soap display. Both women spontaneously ended the silence with: "Well, what do you . . ." and simultaneously stopped and giggled. Finally, Alice took the lead: "Now that a few days have passed, how do you feel about the Gourmet House?"

The two women looked at each other. Actually, they studied each other to decide which one was prettier.

Jennifer had a well shaped body but suffered from a severe case of facial acne. Alice remembered the acne but had not noticed her full shape. Jennifer envied Alice's olive skin although it covered a frail body. Both decided the other was, in total, more attractive. Jennifer answered: "It doesn't bother me so much that I wasn't hired. But, I sure don't expect to be insulted for trying."

"That's exactly what I thought. That's what made me so angry. I've just had it, you know."

"Yea. I think he needs to be tought a lesson, if you ask me."

"Well, that's the reason . . ." Alice started to explain when she heard more visitors at the door. She got up to let them in. "Hello. Wont you come in?"

"Oh, hi. You must be Alice. I'm Connie Ballew and this is Flossy O'Hare."

Connie reached out her hand for Alice to shake. Connie's arms were as big as Alice's thighs and shook like jelly.

"It's nice to meet you although I feel like I already know you after our telephone chat. Hi Flossy. Nice to meet you."

Flossy smiled at the hospitality, exposing a set of partially decayed teeth. She said nothing and appeared reluctant.

Both visitors entered. Connie headed for Jennifer while Flossy studied the apartment, looking for clues. Alice offered the comforts of her home. Finally, Gwen Ryan arrived. Alice made sure everyone had met and served coffee.

After a certain amount of idle chatter, Alice attempted to approach the agenda of their gathering: "O.K., let's talk about why we're here. I think basically it is because we are angry. I know I am. But I'm not sure what to do with my anger. It's sure to be foolish if I do it alone."

"People sh-sh-shouldn't have the r-r-right to be so m-m-mean," Gwen offered as a starter.

"What are rights anyway if you're not rich," answered Jennifer.

Connie's impatience was already showing when she said: "Before we talk about rights, we should decide what we want. I mean personally I'd like to punch his face but that wouldn't do if you know what I mean. Like we should decide if we're trying to get that job for one of us or if we want something from him like money or an appology or something, if you know what I'm saying."

"Well," Alice supported, "that's a good place to start."

"It ought to cost him, that's for sure. An oppology don't mean nothin' to me."

"I agree."

"Me too."

"S-S-Seems right."

"We should decide if we want to just teach him a lesson or if we want something for ourselves," said Connie.

"We could sue him."

"Yea."

"For what?"

"Money!""Yea."

Alice felt apprehensive. I don't like that. I don't want something I didn't earn."

"Alice is right. I don't want his lousy money. He's probably got oodles of it anyway, if you know what I mean," Connie added.

"Then let's get some of it," yelled Jennifer.

"I d-d-don't w-w-want his m-m-money either b-but he shou-shouldn't get away wi-with it."

"That leaves just one course of action and I suggest we. take it."

"What's that, Flossy?"

"We expose him to the public. That way no one can say we're trying to get something for nothing."

Jennifer countered with: "The public don't give a shit."

"Maybe not the public but the law, if you get my point."

"W-w-what law?"

"The OEER. A friend of mine once didn't get a promotion and they hired new guy. She complained to the OEER. They finally made the company promote her. And with back pay."

"That's different though, isn't it? That's sexual discrimination," Alice clarified.

"So is this," Jennifer snapped, "this is as sexual as you can get. I mean nobody even has an idea if we could have done the job. They didn't even care. Mark my word. Whoever they hired will have big bassooms, tan skin and hundreds of sparkling teeth. Ten to one odds on the big tits."

"M-m-must you b-be so c-c-crude?"

"The truth is crude."

"Well, none of us really know the law. We need to talk with a lawyer if we're going to pursue this thing."

"Yea."

"Well then," Connie demanded, "is this the route we're gonna go? We need to decide if you know what I'm saying."

"I th-th-think it's be-be-best."

"So, who knows a lawyer?"

"I do," flaunted Flossy.

"O.K. Will you go talk with him and see what he says?"

"And see what he charges. I don't want this thing ending up costing me an arm and a leg."

"Where are your principles?"

"Where the hell were his?"

"So, what should our argument be?" asked Alice.

"That's what we got lawyers for, if you get my drift."

"I know but I mean we should be able to state the principles which we think have been violated."

"He's a shitass, that's what."

"J-J-Jennifer, p-p-please!"

"Oh, I'm sorry. But it's true."

"It may be but we can't go into court acusing Greenwood of being a shitass if you know what I mean."

Alice laughed. Flossy smiled. Everyone looked down.

"If the law protects our rights, let's figure out what rights were violated."

"Yea."

"Jennifer said it before. It's sexual discrimination. Of sorts."

"But this isn't a contest between male and female."

"Listen kiddo, there's more to sex than what's between your legs."

"Ueh. J-J-Jen"

"I'm sorry—forgive me. I slipped."

"Well, you may be right anyway. It could be considered a kind of sexual discrimination."

"You're right. If we talk about sexuality instead of sex, he still discriminated."

"W-w~which means that w-w-whatever his ownw-w-warped version of s-s-sexiness is, that's wh-wh-who he will hi-hi-hire."

"Right. And it has nothin' to do with how good you can waitress, know what I mean?"

"I think that could be the key. By law—and common decency—he doesn't have the right to not hire us—or one of us—for reasons he admitted are sexual rather than—uhm—real reasons. Like if we didn't have any arms."

"Hey, Flossy, you should'a been takin' notes while the professor was elucidat'n, if you catch my drift."

"I was just trying to sum it up, that's all," Aliee defended.

"She's just joking. I think you summed it up good. I'll talk with the lawyer and see if he can take it from there."

"Now can we eat?" Jennifer pleaded.

CHAPTER 2

THE WRX-TV STUDIO on the north side of Chicago was a technological ant hill. Beings running about in every direction, all appearing to be bred for specific functions. The product of their labor was transient, often disremembered by the consumer within hours of consumption. Some performed their duties in return for essentials, security and identity. Less common were those who saw a purpose in their work. And quite uncommon were those who specifically saw video communication as a means to improving the lot of their fellow beings. No one was permitted by their individual or united mechanisms to see futility.

One of the uncommon beings at WRX-TV was Helen Wells, a political news reporter. She had just received a call from a friend at the Government Printing Office who kept her informally informed of activity at the Capital Ant Hill.

Helen was a busy, determined young lady who sometimes was hard to recognize without a telephone receiver by her face. "I don't believe it," shouting. "How did they justify it. I mean how does this represent people in any way? Or anything except that damn . . . I'm sorry. Why am I yelling at you? How have you been? . . . Hey, that's really great. I hope it turns out better than that last jerk you settled down with . . . No, but I'm patient. No hurry . . . Right. Listen, dear, I have to go. Will you send me a rough copy of the Federal Register while the ink is still wet? . . . Thanks a bunch. Bye, bye."

Helen Wells had been grooming a steadily increasing respect among her peers. This latest project she hoped would accelerate her prospects as an anchor woman. She had a natural image that simply demanded credibility. The simplicity of her phrases, the assumed matter-of-factness and her infatuating smile all contributed to success. A few times she had filled in on the noon talk show with as little as ten minutes notice. Each performance impressed the producer more and also calmed his metabolism which would go berzerk whenever his tempermental talk show hostess did.

After the last incident, Helen was apprehended from her lunch break to do the talk show. Stephanie Rose, the long time star of the show, walked out.

Helen's disappointments hurt Harry to the core. More than once he got drunk over one of Helen's set backs. She, in her naivite, brushed herself off and walked to the next assignment. There was a basic philosophy that seemed to propell Helen Wells. She had an absolute aversion for mediocrity. It was the creators of creativity who she worshipped. She especially favored artists of the conventional oil and canvas. On occasion, Helen dabbled her way to interesting results but she knew basically that paints and brushes were not her element. She was jealous of, and impressed by, successful artists and cultivated their friendship. Art was the most sacred form of expression, in her opinion, and any defamation of its highest possibilities was, if anything was, sinful.

Helen witnessed the first transgression of this sacrament at an artists guild meeting. She attended with a friend. He had paintings on display in several fashionable galleries and one at the Art Institute. Although he was never satisfied with his paintings, Helen admired him for what she considered excellent work. The lecture was to have been about methods of authenticating and restoring old masterpieces. Not enough time remained for its entirety. The preceding business meeting, which normally was five minutes of formality, expanded to thirty minutes. It was condoned with cool indifference and some impatience. There was an air of revolution emanating from the chairman. An absurd intuition, Helen told herself, but there it was. A young man was beating his chest about the plight of starving artists and how society ought to support a certain number of them since they are the uncorrupted visionaries of the world gone by and that yet to come.

It was a disgrace, he said, to have artists live like beggars while floor sweepers and garbage collectors made fifteen dollars an hour. It was high time we treated artists of all persuasions with the respect they deserved. This went on for a bit until he had made his point about five times over. Suddenly his starving look converted to that of a madman with a hidden bomb. He announced with disciplined calm that in fact this inequity was about to come to a halt. He then continued as if all in attendance were initiated co-conspirators. No more than one would discuss hemorroid problems while eating a festive meal in polite company did Helen expect to hear of unionization at an art lecture. Unions were something one dealt with in defined work with definable objectives and procedures; operating machines or building structures. What possible sense could a union of artists make, she wondered. The concept so upset her that, when later she was probed for an opinion of a paint dating technique, Helen finished her coffee, appologized and took leave of her bewildered friends.

That gathering went unnoticed by most. The plagued visions Helen conjured up at that time were now materializing. She noticed a small article about all public supported institutions displaying only contemporary works done by Guild Union artists. The move was supported not only by the local county but by the State legislature. Since this implied mostly the Chicago area, Helen knew where to look next. What she could not grasp at the time was: Why did not anyone oppose this? It was not a chorus of unanimous agreement. It was simply ignored. The real artists, those who had a sincere respect for the art, would no more support unionism than deface a masterpiece.

Shortly after the appearance of that inconspicuous news article, Helen's artist friend, John, called to report that his painting was being removed from the Institute because he did not hold Guild Union membership. When he claimed Guild membership, the difference was explained to him, along with instructions on how to join. He told them where to put that and they in turn told him to remove his. Helen offered her sympathy.

She explained how the issue apparently was not big enough yet to get any media attention. Helen's anger was not only at the Guild Unionists but also at artists like her friend who kept their heads in intellectual, indignant clouds while allowing their footing to erode. Privately, she went into action. Using one of her favarite paintings, she set out to put it on display. Soon she discovered that the Guild Union of Artists was sanctioned by the International Brotherhood of Workers. It was only after the County's endorsement that the Guild Union President was approached by the Brotherhood. He, of course, jumped at the opportunity for national support.

The full impact of this phenomenon did not come to Helen until she obtained an appointment with the Art Institute Director. He was the first man who did not talk about the Brotherhood and dues and starving artists and the public's duty to support a certain element of creative people. Instead, this man spoke of painting style as it were something to regulate. Something about consistency, continuity, predictability. With each word he spoke, the fantasy of horror grew in Helen's reverie, leaving her eyes to open wide. The Director had stopped talking and was offering her a glass of water when she returned to the chair she never left. It seemed to be Helen's style to rise, apologize, and leave whenever her surroundings did not make sense. This she did, but more desperately than usual.

A county was not the nation and Helen decided that this nonsense would soon stop of its own. They were just pseudo artists trying to be paid for their trash. The independent, private galleries would ignore the Union's demands and activities. How could this man be so converted, she wondered? She had credited the Director unconditionally for years with high regard for his performance at the Institute. Now he was the greatest betrayer. It was only petty greed that lured men to pursue unearned wealth. But to prostitute the ideals of creativity and expression was unadorned evil. Such betrayal caught her off guard. If this was possible on a small scale, what might happen when a powerful national union goes to work on the Federal Government?

Maybe she was just being one of those dreaded alarmists. However, the phone call from her Washington friend justified her alarm. It was such achievement which earned Helen the occasional privilege of designing her own talk show program as well as filling in for the newscasters. So far, though, if the anchor man was away, he was always replaced by a regular newscaster. She thought of mentioning this to the assistant producer whose remaining sanity he openly attributed to the spontaneity of Helen. But somehow it did not feel right to Helen to mention it. She guessed there might be some resistance from the three newscasters if a substitute anchored the program. It would not be right to put Harry, the assistant producer, on the spot she decided. Besides, the newsmen were really great guys and very professional. It was frustrating sometimes to be patient while vibrating with ambition.

The nutritionist Stephanie had been interviewing for rehersal hinted at her overweight condition. She ran off the set in a fit of temper. Helen was hurriedly briefed during make-up on the points her guest wanted to make. This left little time for any other discussion. The entire studio was arrested with anxiety as she graciously introduced her puzzled guest. Helen immediately asked him to provide some background about himself. Being an amateur in this field, Helen asked the very questions a viewer might have asked. By the time she remembered the four points to be brought out, she realized three had already been covered while the forth turned out to be good summary conversation. One second after the camera's red light went off, all manner of studio hands, camera men and executives broke the seriousness with jubilant applause. A confused guest sort of smiled, mumbled an uncertain 'Thank you' while Helen remained seated and smiled.

Creativity, credibility and caring. That was Mr. Seegraph's apparent motto because he would recite the 'Three Cs' to disapprove of a particular news segment which he determined was not up to par. Helen thought frequently about these attributes and consciously tried to incorporate them in her work. She would have added a fourth 'C' to the motto—curiosity. A skill that Helen had to offer was the ability to combine seemingly unrelated bits of information and turn them into a story before it should have been a story. Several times already the executive producer had called, wondering how the hell they scooped an event when no one appeared to be assigned. The queries would wind up with Harry, who always had the same answer. If Harry had a daughter of twenty-five, she would have been just like Helen, he decided.

He never let her know how he felt. He wanted her to struggle and feel every bit of pain, frustration and disappointment this career had to offer.

CHAPTER 3

FLOSSY O'HARE WAS elected Secretary/Treasurer at their second public meeting. Also decided was the group's name. F-A-I-R. They agreed they would come up with words for the acronyn later.

In the excecutive meeting that followed immediately after the public meeting, Flossy was nominated to permanently represent FAIR to their attorney. She accepted with a giggle. Having been a legal secretary for nearly three years, she felt quite confident in this first assignment.

A complaint was filed with the Office of Equal Employment Responsibility against Mr. Richard A. Greenwood, owner and manager of Gourmet house, Green Bay, Wisconsin. The charging parties were: The President, the Vice-President for Public Relations, the Vice-President for Membership, the Secretary/Treasurer and the Executive Director, Ms. Alice Trevon, of FAIR.

With membership over fifty and growing at ten dollars annual dues, mostly collected, FAIR could afford a good lawyer. Tom Stuart, Esquire, was offered the job. He specialized in accidents and divorce but FAIR sounded like fun. And besides, Greenwood called him a sonofabitch in court when he represented a client that cut himself falling off a broken toilet seat. The case left the jury in stitches and Greenwood paying a $1500 liability.

When Greenwood received his hearing notice, he called Stuart to let him know there were no hard feelings from the last encounter:

"That's O.K. Tom. I don't give a shit. I'm glad it's an open hearing. I'll even invite the press. My clientel will double when the newspapers tell them we have the best looking women working for us. And look, Tom, when people see that litter of dogs you represent, they'll either barf or laugh. Anyway, just so you don't get too cocky, I've got one card up my sleeve."

"Lookin' forward to it. See ya."

While the OEER hearing was to be FAIR's revolutionary battle, much more had to be done to gain strength. They had to increase their membership. At home they would grow by word of mouth; especially after the publisized OEER hearing. To spread to other areas, the consensus strategy was to contact friends in other cities. A distribution list was started. Someone became the mailing expert. Another was delegated to the important task of designing a starter kit. These would ultimately be mailed to those friends who agreed to set up similar organizations in their cities. Within a month, FAIR had chapter in Wichita, Flint, Trenton and Seattle. With ten percent of the dues being returned to the home office, now called **FAIR NATIONAL HQ**, their expansion grew even faster. Tom Stuart was so busy keeping FAIR, Inc. compatible with the laws, that he dropped everything else. The executives of FAIR took turns flying to those cities which looked promising. The dues collected at each meeting or rally usually paid for the trip and sent money dribbling in. In less than a half year, FAIR had a membership of 5000 and was about to pass into the big time.

A trial date for the Greenwood case was set. The fact finding hearing left both sides unmoved with no amicable resolution likely. FAIR's Public Relations Vice-President sent news releases to several papers and broadcast stations. One such release came to WRX-TV. While Helen was looking for a script on Harry's desk, she read:

UNFAIR HIRING policy goes to court. Green Bay, Wisconsin. Richard Greenwood, owner/ manager of the Gourmet House has been charged with illegal hiring policies. A rapidly growing organization called FAIR, Inc. headquartered in Green Bay, has brought suit against Greenwood for not hiring one of five women who interviewed for a job last July. The charges include violations of OEER regulations such as sexual discrimination, failure to show cause why he did not hire one of the interviewed women, all of whom now head the FAIR organization, and defamation of character. Greenwood reportedly called the five ladies a "truckload of dogs". He has continued to refuse hiring anyone who does not meet his criteria of appearance. A trial has been set for November 17.

There was not enough information to go on but Helen felt an overpowering urge to visit Green Bay and check out the story. The only thing she had ever heard of Green Bay was a football team and Fort Howard Paper Company. She always wondered if there was anything else to this little city.

CHAPTER 4

PROBABLY THE MOST outstanding reason Rucker, Snells & Associates were awarded the advertising contract for Catherine Products' new line of lipstick was their reputation for predicting consumer trends, Someone paid this compliment to Dean Rucker years ago and he decided to capitalize on it. He recently hired Nancy McGee, a young lady who had graduated with honors in sociology, read like lightning and had good retention. She had been with Rucker and Snells for the past two years and spent nearly all of her time scanning newspapers and magazines. Not just the major publications but also a few obscure tabloids which would reflect the life of more remote communities.

Robert Snells grew up in the farm lands of northeast Wisconsin and consequently was a Green Bay Packer football fanatic. The Green Bay Tribune always served two purposes. Nancy McGee forwarded the sports section to Bob while she scanned the rest. She happened to notice the write up of a trial, two days old now, which had the hints of a legend being born.

Reportedly, a Mr. Greenwood defended himself at a trial for an OEER case. He was charged with five counts of unfair hiring practices among other indiscretions. Mr, Greenwood's assistant had prepared a survey of one thousand restaurant patrons. The participants had to choose one of two hypothetical restaurants. Given the service and food was of the same quality, the choice was actually between photographs of two groups of waitresses. One group was comprised of attractive women while the other illustrated ladies from plain to unsightly. It was pointed out that the personalities of all waitresses were to be considered pleasant with only the cosmetic appearances varying. The survey results, along with the visual aids were entered into the record. The survey implied that 83% of regular restaurant patrons preferred to be waited on by attractive ladies and would be influenced thus in their choice of restaurants. Excactly half of the participants were female. Mr. Greenwood argued that other businesses generally have the right to hire employees based on their possession of important skills and physical attributes. Agility, muscular strength and responsibility Mr. Greenwood stated were necessary attributes for the moving and storage business if such a company was to provide the type of service desired by their clients. Forcing them to change their hiring policy would eliminate the ability to compete and damage a lot of furniture.

Mr. Greenwood made the entire delivery without once looking at the charging parties or their legal council. When the second charge was brought forth, that the defendant had referred to the plaintiffs as a "truckload of dogs", Mr. Greenwood delivered his coup de grace. He calmly stated that he exercised every courtesy in the presence of these ladies during the inteview and that he had a right to his personal opinion; that in fact these ladies were guilty of eavesdropping on a private conversation and he intended to pursue legal action at the conclusion of this trial.

The Judge ultimately decided the case was without merit. The plaintiffs' attorney, T. Stuart, announced the decision would be appealed.

*   *   *

Nancy McGee leaned back and visualized a shingle reading RUCKER, SNELLS, McGEE & ASSOCIATES. Getting the Catherine Products lipstick account was a breakthrough in their first large industry. Rucker and Snells were on trial and, if found competent, might gain a larger portion of Catherine Products' advertising budget.

Cosmetics was a subject Dean had always wanted to dabble in. It offered such colorful possibilities (and some interesting models). Nancy had an idea how she could land the entire Catherine Products account and perhaps even a few others. She phoned to make an appointment with someone from FAIR, Inc. A meeting was set for the following week.

*　　*　　*

"Harry, you should have seen that trial," beamed Helen mischievously.

"You found another villain?"

"I'm not sure what I found. But what I saw were some bitter, pathetic women who certainly weren't attractive but their real ugliness was in their demeanor. It was like they expected something to compensate for their physical appearnces. Greenwood just happened to be the punch bag."

"So, what was his defense? Did he admit the charge?"

"No, he didn't and . . . oh! We'll have another please . . . and I'm paying for these . . . anyway, although he seemed a bit crude, he was no fool. He simply used a survey to show what people wanted and explained that it was his business to give it to them. He almost was charged with contempt when he told the judge that the legal system should concentrate on punishing people that try to take things away rather than those who earn their way honestly. Most of the time he talked right at the judge. He was a sight. Especially when he accused the women of eavesdropping. Greenwood was abrasive and a real chauvinist at heart but he had a good argument and that's what was on trial." Deciding she needed to breathe, Helen gave Harry a chance to respond.

"So, did he win?"

"Oh, philosophically—yes. Hands down. But they'll appeal and that may become a different matter."

"Why,' he baited Helen, "if he has a good argument?"

"Oh, don't be so naive. This isn't high school civics." A little too sharp, Helen decided and looked down at her drink. Harry knew the impatience was not for him.

"You're all hyper. What's really bothering you?"

"It's this FAIR organization, Harry. The plaintiffs from the trial are the executives. In a few months—just a few months—they grew from nothing to seven thousand. I'm sure their anger gave them lots of energy at first. But seven thousand people, Harry? Giving twenty dollars to belong to what? What are their goals? It's not isolated.

Did you read the rough draft of the report I turned in today on the Artists' Union?"

"Glanced at it. I'll go over it tonight if you don't get me plastered."

"Then you're cut off now because I want you to read it. I want to know if you get the same sickening feelings I got from writing it. It's not isolated, Harry. There is growing sickness. It's not my imagination. We're talking about potentially powerfull groups. National groups. Guided by philosophies that that . . . aren't even philosophies. More like amoral opportunism. I don't know"

"Hey," Harry broke in, "you're getting hysterical. Listen . . . I think you have a point. But let's do this. Instead of just zeroing in on the Guild Union of Artists, why don't you work up a general approach? I'll bring it up to Seegraph. A deal?"

"Oh, thank you, Harry." Helen stood up, wrapped her arms around Harry and kissed him on his forehead.

"I guess I'll go soak in the tub. Good night."

"Thanks for putting up with me."

Harry just gave her a wink. He sat and thought for a while and decided she had a good idea.

CHAPTER 5

FAIR INCORPORATED MOVED their headquarters from an old house on the south side of Green Bay to downtown. A two thousand square foot area was leased on the first floor of the Water Place Inn. The local group was growing larger and always there were visitors at the monthlies. It did not make sense to lease enough area for the monthlies, the President decided, as they would always have access to one of the large banquet rooms.

Their headquarters, or HQ as Connie Ballew liked to call it, was modestly attired. The only enclosed office was given to Alice since she now worked full time and was salaried. There was a rest room, a soft drink machine, open shelves and four work tables. Upon first entering one would be reminded of a temporary war game room for a military maneuver. A strategy map on the windowless wall depicted various concentrations of memberships by color coded dots. Access to this comprehensive map was gained by makeshift rolling steps.

The FAIR officers did most of the travelling. Alice could not really see herself conducting one of those FAIR rallies but still wondered what it would be like. She was more comfortable behind the scenes anyway. Although it was one of the volunteers who one night nick-named this the War Room, Alice agreed that it did look like one and had a sign indicating the same. Amidst all her thinking, an uncomfortable feeling began gnawing on her mind but she was barely conscious of it. Perhaps, Alice thought, it looked more like a political party campaign headquarters. Something, however, was misssing. A motto. That is what was needed. The organization's name sort of implied their motto but it was incomplete. Fair about what?

Alice recalled what had started it all last year. All she wanted was a job. She could have learned it quickly. Instead they hired a beauty. That thought struck a spark. The crux of the matter, Alice quickly concluded, was that by a quirk of nature she was being denied the good feeling that came from being pretty. Men falling all over themselves to do things for you. It was not just the silly job that mattered. When the Appeals Court overruled the Circuit Court on the OEER decision, Greenwood was forced to offer a waitress job to one of the plaintiffs. After the appeal trial, FAIR offered to drop the matter if Greenwood dropped the invasion of privacy suit. So it was settled. No one wanted the job anyway. Not with their new status. The officers became jetsetters and Alice was and felt—important, looked up to and depended upon. But, she still wanted what that waitress got the first night and paid her a dollar fifty more. It was not fair. Alice thought she could have been just as good for the job. What do breasts have to do with serving food? Nothing. They get in the way if anything. Then Alice remembered that humiliating trial. Their lawyer had almost guaranteed them a victory. She remembered how torn she felt when Greenwood presented his argument and that survey. She was almost inclined to agree with him for a moment but then realized that what he presented is not what people should want. It should not matter. People go to estaurants to eat food—not to oogle at beautiful waitresses. They can go to a strip joint for that. That was why the membership was growing so rapidly. Even without a motto, FAIR was what many people had been waiting for. Its message was implied if not spoken. It was not just fairness. Or even rights, although that could not be seperated. Alice finally came to the apex of her thoughts; to the word without which she had become increasingly ill-at-ease the past weeks. The word was: Equity. What good were jobs, what good was money, what good was anything, if some man did not admire her for herself. She was thinking with the momentum of an avalanche. And even women, she quickly corrected her thoughts, because she was intent on keeping this philosophically pure. If we were really born equal, as even our Constitution states, then we should enjoy the same benefits. Otherwise, what's the use of being equal? Tangible. The same same FEELINGS. Equal feelings.

No, not benefits. That was it. True equality. With that conclusion, Alice fumbled for a note pad to become a one woman think tank. Some of the slogans she produced were: EQUALITY FOR EVERYONE. No, too vague. A RIGHT TO EQUALITY. Good, but didn't say enough. It would have to stand up to arguments. Alice could not resist writing UGLY PEOPLE NEED LOVING TOO. That was the difficulty. The motto could not deny the obvious. Some people were more attractive than others. WE'RE ALL ATTRACTIVE SOMEHOW. No. She could see crude people like Mr. Greenwood defacing their posters. It had to be something she could announce with pride—even to an audience of crude listeners. Something not even they could deny. She recalled overhearing one of the most offensive statements in her life. A worker from a road crew shouted: 'Stand them on their heads and they're all alike'. "Disgusting," she said out loud. And yet, philosophically, in a more sophisticated way of course, it actually was a sound statement. Just too limited. Now, if one could refer to the whole person instead of the obsession with sex organs, Alice thought, there might be a good motto. It must have dignity, warmth and, of course, equality. At the thought of those parameters, she watched her hand write, as if on a Ouija board: WE'RE ALL THE SAME INSIDE. "That's it," she yelled to the absent platoon outside. "And that takes care of whose picture we would use, No one's. I mean, everyone's." Her mind synthesised a conglomerate of people – some beautiful, others not beautiful, with arms draped around each other. All are smiling and feeling good. Underneath would be the caption: WE'RE ALL THE SAME INSIDE.

There, Alice decided. She certainly earned her keep today. Who needs Rucker and Snells or whoever Connie was meeting with today? This was the grassroots of real equality, she insisted. Not an ad agency. With this, she smartly picked up her purse, tossed her brown bag into the trash can and treated herself to an executive lunch.

CHAPTER 6

I T WAS SATURDAY. A pleasant, cloudless sky outside but Nancy McGee was at her desk. She always went there to think. Like some people do in a large, empty cathedral. The advertising business inspired the same kind of awe in her. There was a sense of creativity and power in helping people to choose certain products over others. A multimillion dollar industry could be brought to its knees by competitive advertising, Men, machines and products mattered nothing if the whimsical preference of consumers could be influenced to a different brand, a new concept or a better life style. The promise of this world kept Nancy's mind craving for new ideas while her friends were busy amusing themselves with water sports and picnics.

She hated to turn down their invitation but knew her mind would have been preoccupied with the idea of cosmic equality. The trends were clear enough. It was not that fat slob's charisma that generated a membership of 11,200 in so little time. Nancy understood power, subtle or raw. She thought of herself as a sociological judo expert. Find the power, someone else's, and its direction. Before it gains too much momentum it will respond to moderate attitude correction. Divert power through the right chanels and capitalize on its momentum. Like diverting a stream over a water wheel.

Nancy did not yet know how to tap this power but stood first in line offering assistance to FAIR while its leaders still felt they needed assistance. She could see that their President was not aware of the force they had released.

While wars and social program appealed to only some, self-esteem was a concern of everyone. Her thoughts lept about like this until she noticed Dean Rucker arriving at the parking lot. This was the right time, Nancy concluded, with a shot of adrenalin reddening her cheeks.

"Dean, what are you doing here?" The question seemed to come from a superior.

"What am I doing here? Why you little wippersnapper. Who are you earning brownie points for?" Dean could get away with this familiarity because he openly recognized Nancy's potential. Bob Snells, more leery of her abilities and motives, was relegated by an unspoken agreement to a more distant relationship.

"I'm plotting to take over the agency and that kind of work is always done on ones own time." This came out without benefit of forethought followed by a desperate search for a different subject.

"Plotting, eh? You know my mother always said to me . . . I know you hate cliches . . . she said that whenever someone makes a joke, there's always a bit of truth in it."

Nancy was startled as if she had been caught embezzling funds. That is why she respected—no, admired—Dean Rucker. He was the only person who could see right through her, good or bad. No sense trying to cover up now, she thought, and regained control of the conversation: "Well then, let me tell you about the little bit of truth. Do you have time?"

"Oh, sure. I don't even know why I'm here. Mary's still asleep and the kids went camping. Just restless, I guess."

"You too, huh? You really like your work, don't you?"

"Most of the time."

"When don't you?" She said this with half interest and half preparation.

"When we lose a contract bid."

"Let's talk about winning one." Nancy swallowed involuntarily.

"Oh yea? Shoot, sport."

"I want to become a full partner."

Dean's body functions stopped momentarily. "Christ, you don't go for subtlety, do you?"

"Not when I'm "scared," Nancy answered.

"You have been like a strung bow this week. Are you upset about something?"

"No, no. I just want to be a partner, I mean you really didn't know my career objectives, did you? At least, you never asked,"

"I knew what they weren't," Dean defended.

"Well, that is what they are. Now let me tell you what I'll try to do to earn it," Dean was frozen to his chair and posture, staring at Nancy.

"O.K?" she asked, realizing this most important answer implied whether the position could even be earned.

"Yea, yea. Don't keep me waiting with triffles."

Now the battle was half won and to Nancy this was most assuredly a battle. "Good. If I delivered the entire Catherine Products account, would that be an adequate initiation fee?"

"Good God . . ," Dean muttered although he was an atheist.

"Well, don't sound like I planned to knock off the Chase Manhatten. Besides, I haven't done it yet."

"YET," Dean screamed, "she says YET. We've been trying for two years and she says yet and I'm pissed because I know she can do it even though I don't know how—yet." The window received most of this.

"Quite a monologue."

"Quite a project . . . Let me recover by getting us some coffee. Be right back." Deans departure left Nancy to enjoy the warm glow of a vote of confidence. Every bit as warm as the sun outside.

CHAPTER 7

A N ORDER FOR a fifteen second spot, to be telecast at WRX-TV before the six and ten news, was forwarded to the programmer. The spot was already video taped and needed only the audio updated. Helen was just passing the program studio when she noticed a still image on the monitor. It depicted a gathering of jovial people with the inscription WE'RE ALL THE SAME INSIDE at the bottom of the scene. Helen entered the studio. The programmer waved her to silence and started to scream into the microphone from a script that called for screaming. Carefully she closed the door and stood motionless, listening. "Are you tired of missing out on life because the arbitrary hand of nature didn't make you glamorous? If you would like to be involved with an organization that is trying to educate our society, fight for equality and promote the internal beauty of everyone, then you are being called to attend a FAIR rally on Wednesday evening, eight o'clock, on the seventh floor of the Conrad Hilton. A get acquainted party with free champagne while it lasts will follow a lecture by Dr. Phillip Wheaton, titled IS BEAUTY SKIN DEEP? Remeber, that's Wednesday night, eight o'clock at the Conrad Hilton." The programmer was out of breath, glanced at the clock and hissed in a completely different voice: "Shit, that's twenty seconds." "What's the matter, Al? Trying to squeeze ten pounds into a five pound bag?"

"Wash your mouth. Actually, you're right . . . and it is shit that I'm trying to squeeze." Al glanced at the script again in disbelief. "Goddamn, for all the money they're raking in, you'd think they could pay for a thirty second spot and let me breathe once. Anyway, can I help you, beautiful?"

"You just have," Helen replied, dashed out of the studio and left Al more bewildered than usual. "Harry! Harry, where are you?" She was opening doors, offering excuse me's until she found Harry sitting in a lounge seat, calmly waiting to be found.

"Hey, quiet down. Do you want to give away my hiding place?" Harry would always offer teasing therapy for a hyperventilating Helen.

"You stinker. I'll report you immediately to your supervisor."

"Oh, please, no. Anything but that. I'd have to find out which one of them is my supervisor."

"O.K. I'll let you off easy. I'll settle for someone else covering the story on the bond issue debate Wednesday night."

"What could possibly be happening to distract you from such an important, intriguing civic event?"

"There is a FAIR rally I want to attend. I mean, cover. I haven't really seen them in action since they became so prominent."

"What a coincidence. It just happened that Ernie was reassigned to cover the bond issue thing so he could get home by nine."

"And when was that re-assignment made?" Helen asked with feigned indignation.

"Oh, Friday. A few minutes after we received an order to do a fifteen second spot for FAIR."

"You're a sweetheart. Thank you."

"This isn't a boondoggle. You'll be there to work." Harry had difficulty pulling off a stearn demeanor.

"Right, chief." Helen saluted and left.

*   *   *

Helen arrived early at the Conrad Hilton. She didn't wear her press pass but reserved a seat near the front by placing her program brochure in it. She went back down to the lobby, took a quick glance at the display of oils and acryllics in the lobby and headed for the Haymarket Lounge. The three dollar investment in a Tom Collins gave Helen access to conversations on each side of her. Both were quite audible and dealt with the anticipated lecture. In the conversation at the bar, many calories were being wasted by three people shouting at each other.

In the process, none of them apparently recognized they were all saying the same thing. Another debate held more promise. Here were two ladies chatting amiably, with only token sounds coming from the captured gentleman standing between them.

"But don't you think a woman has more influence over her life if she's attractive?" asked one.

The other twinkled back: "That's just the point, my dear. Why should an attractive woman have more rights than an unattractive one?"

"But they don't," was the answer, "they simply manage to influence more effectively."

"By what right?" was demanded, somewhat haughty by then.

"I don't see where it is a matter of rights. It is simply reality."

"It's also reality for some people to kill and steal but we don't permit such conduct."

"And it continues to happen because that is the reality of human nature." Helen soon grew weary of the circle of arguments and wondered what their gentleman was thinking about. The first time he moved anything was his head to watch Helen leave.

Helen's impromptu seat reservaion was respected. She wanted to be near the front to catch the facial innuendo of the speaker as well as the response of the audience. She sat herself down and patiently waited for the program to begin. The quiet man in the Lounge turned out to be Dr. Wheaton. He caught her gaze immediately and looked at her for an eternity of ten seconds. He then returned his attention to the stage and did not find Helen again for the remainder of the congress.

An attractive master of ceremonies approached the microphones, welcomed the audience and guests and introduced the FAIR President, Connie Ballew. What Connie felt and what she conveyed were not alike. Ever since the possibilities of FAIR were pointed out by Ms. McGee, she felt like a bewildered little child whose meddling caused a concrete truck to start rolling down a hill. She had read the outline of the speech Dr. Wheaton was about to give and was dumbfounded at his implications.

Yet, she had to remind herself that this is what they wanted. Connie missed the feeling of control even though in fact, formally, she still was at the helm. That is what she portrayed when she introduced Dr. Wheaton. This was the man, credentials and all, who happens to exactly represent our views, Connie implied, as she turned the Doctor loose.

Dr. Wheaton stood up from his chair of honor and rushed to the microphones like a sesoned graduate of think positive training: "Ladies and Gentlemen. It is indeed a pleasure to be here tonight. When Ms. Ballew invited me to speak to the title of IS BEAUTY SKIN DEEP, I was both astounded and delighted. I have spent many years in the research laboratories of leading cosmetic firms. Some of my work went toward applied cosmetics that were also good for the skin. As you can see, I have been devoted to skin deep beauty for much of my life. And yet, I'm just like any of you. I go to work and I go home. In my daily associations I meet all kinds of people and there is one thing for certain: You have to look beyond the surface for the real person. Of course, anything below the surface is really out of my professional realm but certainly not disconnected."

"For example, diet is very important to the way you look and so is your vitality. And your attitude. So, I think you can see that I truly am delighted to be able to talk about the whole person. In fact, this is probably the first time I'm not speaking from a purely professional platform and am feeling quite excited."

"So, how does skin deep beauty coexist with the motto WE'RE ALL THE SAME INSIDE? Quite well actually and this is why: When we look at someone, we see mainly their body covering and their shape. And especially their face. However, in order for skin and shape to have any meaning at all, we also need the entire rest of the body. Many organs and pathways and most importantly, a brain. No one cares the least about how these appear aesthetically. In fact, remove and display anyone of these organs seperately and most of us would become ill at thier sight. But in their place and properly functioning, they have their own beauty. Since only the function and not the looks are important, we can honestly say that we are all the same inside. Of course we all think differently and our organs have their individual traits but their purpose is generally the same. And that purpose is to support a mind that is trying to be happy. Everyone may choose a different way to be happy but they are all beautiful because they are trying. This is a pervasive beauty we're talking about. Much more important than the centerfold type of beauty. For example, just imagine someone exceedingly beautiful but helplessly drunk for whatever reason. She regurgitates into her dinner plate. Is she still beautiful? I think not. Not until she reconnects effectively with the pursuit of happiness. Take anyone of you out there. I assume—and hope—for my own vanity that you came here tonight voluntarily. You may have been motivated by something that doesn't please you, either about yourself or your social environment. Well, the important thing is that you came. You're trying. To learn. To understand. To discover how other people think. That, I think, is a very beautiful act."

"Have I told you anything you didn't already know? Of course not. Unless we're talking about chemicals and compounds and skin tones, I have no more claim to expertise on this subject than you. However, I spent the last three nights outlining what I wanted to say and that puts me three days ahead of you. Well, I was a little scared when I started but am feeling quite comfortable now. Any of you who would like to be up here instead of me will have an opportunity in a short while to prove it. I want you to think of this for a moment. Perhaps I'll call on one of you to join me. It's lonely up here. Did some of you just feel a flush of fear? Most of you for one reason or another would probably rather I did not call on you. Raise your hand if you disagree." No hands were visible but there was some giggling. "One of the reasons of reluctance might be that you think you don't look like you should or want. Well, look at me. I'll give you a chance to really giggle while I quench my thirst. Now, think of it. I'm going bald, my abdomen is too large and I have corns. Hardly a sex symbol. Yet I'm not very conscious of my imperfections. Even after pointing them out. This is especially for you ladies now: Look at how men somehow have connived society to ignore for the most part how they look, especially their legs, and pay more attention to things they do, say or think and the amount of money they get for it. In other words—things they can control. Of course, since they've only recently shared the drivers seat with women, they've had many years to condition us. While you women have gained your rights to be employed based on what you can do, say or think, you haven't accomplished such objectivity on the social scene. But that demonstrates what FAIR is all about. FAIR goes beyond just trying to secure your rights. They speak to all of humanity and in all situations. Not just employment but every interaction with other humans. They are trying with their various activities to educate our society toward more objective relationships. If learning is beautiful, then FAIR is certainly making our Country more beautiful. But, there lurks a stubborn segment of our society. Try as we may, some will adhere to their prejudices. They will still judge on purely physical attributes."

"Some of us here tonight still have some of that conditioning left even though we may have surpassed it intellectually. Alow me to demonstrate."

The room darkened. A split screen reflected the images of two women. One very beautiful; the other quite grotesque but with some similarity to the first. "Now, take a look at these two ladies. First, let me point out as some of you suspected that they are one and the same person. I chose this example to illustrate our own prejudices. The woman in this photo was involved in an automobile accident where her face was severely lacerated, jaw bones broken, one eye lost with burns to most of her face. This woman was an attractive interior decorator with growing prominence in the Miami area. She had a wealth of friends, sizeable income, a glamorous life. She was twenty-eight and beautiful at the time of her accident. That was ten years ago. She has undergone thirty-two sessions of reconstructive surgery. During that time she has used up her considerable savings, has attempted suicide three times, has not been able to find work and was only sustained by her partnership in a small furniture store. In the last year, she made a significant turn around following some helpful breakthroughs in prosthetic devices. She now works again, has a social life and has had several offers of marriage. Please take a look at the next slide and compare the tremendous improvements provided by extensive and expensive cosmetic surgery." Several 'wows' were audible.

"Think for a moment about your own reactions as your mind passed the sequence of the slides . . . from the first . . . to the second . . . to the third slide. How would you have responded to this woman if she were standing, facing you, in a crowded elevator? Difficult to handle for most of us, I suspect. If I've made my point, allow me to go on. This woman's recovery is as remarkable as was the severity of the damage she incurred. It required much courage and money. Others less fortunate do not always have sufficient quantities of one or the other—or both."

"I'm going to show you some more slides before introducing a very special guest. Please note your reaction to different accidents, deformations and aesthetic aberrations and see which affect you the most. For those holding their breath, relax. The slides will not be gory but fairly normal occurences."

The slides faded in and out alternately on the two screens. Helen soon felt the point Dr. Wheaton was trying to make. Dr. Wheaton continued: "1 think by now most of you have noted how important an unblemished face is to our society. Missing limbs, eye patches, deformed hands, hunch backs and many other forms of pityful faults are not nearly as disturbing as facial abnormalities. Even minor problems, if located near the mouth, nose or eyes. The face, with its multitude of muscles and features express our innerself more intensely than any other part of our body. In most societies it is also more likely to be exposed than any other body parts. Of the face, the eyes are the epicenter of expression and communication. They provide an intensity of response so intimate that strangers are rarely able to indulge in such a look for more than a few seconds. When a face is disfigured, the normal rules of expressive communication no longer apply. People respond with fear, anger, pity, shame; anything but normal. The unfortunate person with such a problem is looking for such responses because that is the pattern they've usually experienced. This tends to amplify any deviation from normal response and ultimately cause the victim to become introverted, hostile, negative and antisocial. Once on this course, it is most difficult to reverse the trend."

"With that background, let me bring out our special guest, Mr. David Whiting. He will explain his own condition as well as the source of it. Please welcome Mr. Whiting." Dr. Wheaton lead the applause followed enthusiastically by the audience. After a few seconds of Mr. Whiting's appearance, the applause slowed to an occasional crackling.

Mr. Whiting was ugly beyond sufficient description. One eye protruded. Most of the visible skin was discolored with some bright patches of purple. The nostrils were virtually verticle with only a hint of a nose. Part of Mr. Whiting's face was paralized causing the left side of his already extremely thick lower lip to droop. He apparently was unable to control his saliva from this side of his mouth. He had to continuously dab his mouth with a handkechief. His voice appeared high pitched in relation to his bulk. He proceded to describe his condition, the quality of his life. Although he never finished high school, he escaped into books and had a measured I.Q. of 158. He talked of his sexual frustrations, his social and occupational void. Finally he explained that the funds from his appearance at this lecture would be his first hope of corrective surgery. For most of his life he had worked at minimum pay jobs, almost always involving no people contact. Generally, the slightest reason to dismiss him would be invoked repeatedly. He held over fifty jobs in the last twenty years. His last comment was to say that he still did not hate people.

Mr. Whiting's face was glistening, mostly from the hot lights. Dr. Wheaton stepped in by placing his hand on Whiting's shoulder and said: "Dave, I really want to thank you for talking to us. I wont presume to fathom the courage it rquired of you but sincerely hope that this is the beginning of a better life for you. Thank you." Whiting put his head down, nodded once and walked off the platform.

The audience was absolutely motionless. Those who came to be entertained—were. Those who came to feel—did.

Those who were confused became determined. Helen stopped making notes.

Dr. Wheaton continued, "Ladies and Gentlemen, I hope no one was offended by what we arranged. What better way to ask: Does Dave Whiting have the right to a better life than the exile he has felt? So, while FAIR is trying to educate society, we might meet it partway. Let's take a second look at what options we really have. Now I'm speaking to you as a professional. I can tell you that there are many cosmetic services and products available. Some seem ahead of their time. Some of these of course are kept off the market because they would upset the cosmetic industry too much. However, if there was an incentive to do so, any product you can conceive of would probably be produced. From the lay person's point of view, there are three limitations: One, we don't know everything that is available. Two, we don't know how to use what is available most effectively. And three, we often can't afford it. I'm sure you know that cosmetic improvement can involve complicated surgery. This is very expensive. Although some medical insurances cover some cosmetic surgery, much of our knowledge goes unapplied to all but the wealthiest."

"NOW, most of you are here tonight because you espouse a certain philosophy about the concept of beauty and relationships. The fact remains that even after years of successful campaigning, FAIR will not stamp out prejudice. This translates into the physically beautiful people still getting the beautiful jobs, beautiful friends, and beautiful incomes. The fact remains that there are unhappy people. Like Dave Whiting. Unhappy not just about how they look but what their appearance has denied them. The list of injustices is long and sad. What good is wealth if you're unhealthy, some have asked? I ask: What good is health, wealth, fame, or anything, if you're lonely, unhappy, discouraged? That is not to say that good health and a good income isn't important. In our affluent society, we've been able to guarantee at least a minimum of income and health care to our more unfortunate citizens. But, if the benefits of health and wealth are undermined for a sector of unhappy people whose only obstacle to getting the little they want out of life is that they don't look physically attractive—or at least acceptable—then it's time to look at priorities. Our Government exists to serve us. It can do more than keep our organs healthy. If FAIR's rapid growth reflects what aware citizens are asking for; if FAIR can divert some of our thinking from the outside to the inside; then our Government can divert some of its funds from taking care of the inside to taking care of the outside. If cosmetic services were available to not only the priviledged wealthy; if more people knew of the services being suppressed by greedy industries; then with the help of FAIR members, we could truly help make this a more beautiful world." Before the end of the word 'beautiful', the audience lept to their feet and applauded heartily to demonstrate their united support. "Thank you. Thank you very much. All of you, It's been a real pleasure. And now, let me turn the floor back over to your President, Ms. Ballew."

Chapter 8

J UST LIKE CLOCKWORK. Nancy McGee left the phone booth . . . walked two blocks east and entered the lobby of Catherine Products Central Office Building. Five minutes remained. Ample time to freshen up and arrive on the twelfth floor, she thought. A receptionist greeted Nancy with directions to the conference room. She heard men's voices in disciplined debate through the open door. She knocked to transfer the responsibility of intoductions to one of them.

"Ahh, this must be our Miss McGee now," announced a gentleman from the far end of the table.

"That I am but plese call me Nancy. Good morning to you all." "Good morning," said an uncoordinated chorus.

"You've stirred up quite a mystery which only our Chairwoman seems to know the clues to," said another, hinting for one more clue.

"I hope to replace the mystery with a healthy alliance but I shouldn't discuss it further until we've formally begun." This stopped further attempts at baiting. Nancy was offered a seat at one end of a twelve person table by the man most likely to make the first pass at her. The others found their seats and fumbled with their agenda lists.

Since this was a special board meeting, the second this month, the only agenda item was the McGee presentation.

Such billing created a reverence which allowed Nancy the solitude to discover the lack of masculine decor normally found in a conference room. Bamboo wallpaper, a plentiful selection of plants, an aerial photo of probably their original manufacturing plant and a painting of a stately man with long sideburns and 1920's attire.

As Catherine Brenner entered, everyone stood, including Nancy.

Mrs. Brenner was a large woman, mid-sixties; brownish, short, straight hair; tweed suit. Interestingly to Nancy, she practiced the most subtle use of makeup that helped her to look about fifty. The purposeful manner of her stride took a few more years off any estimate. "Good morning, good morning. Please sit down. Nice to see you, Miss HcGee. Have you met everyone?"

Mrs. Brenner sounded more like she was entering her own kitchen.

"Good morning to you, No, not everyone."

"Good. I love to show them off, They may act gentle but are an impressive team of ambition, intelligence and looks. Not a pot belly in the room. Except for mine perhaps. So, this is Roger Thornton Duane Beckman . . . ."

For all their credentials, Nancy thought they looked like sheep but looks could be deceiving. It remained her main objective to convince Mrs. Brenner. The rest would probably follow. ". . . and Sam Meier. Gentlemen, Nancy McGee who promises to be a shrewd challenge. If no one has any objections, I'd like to get on with the meeting. Five minutes for Nancy's proposal. Five minutes for questions to Nancy. Five more to decide, during which my dear I'd like for you to wait outside, and a final minute to announce our decision and set a time for negotiating a contract if such is to follow. Any questions? . . . Good. Shall we begin, Miss McGee?"

Nancy was glad that Mrs. Brenner used her last name. She began her proposal from a colorful set of prepared charts. It was a very ambitious plan, even for Catherine Products. Two new preperation and bottling lines would have to be added as well as an entire division to handle the software programs. The insight to this comprehensive plan was made possible by Dr. Wheaton's experience. The Board of Directors felt cumulative alarm at an outsider having such a detailed knowledge of their production capabilities and limitations.

When the entire promotion package was presented, Nancy added some extra comments to pave the way for acceptance: "Let me remind you of the reason consumers say Pampers, Trampoline or Kleenex. These are all brand names but used synonomously by most people to describe a product made by many industries. The reason for this is that they were the first brand. While other industries were playing catch-up, the original manufacturers were already developing product loyalty that still exists in many cases today. If you can be the first to offer a comprehensive cosmetic regimen shortly after a government subsidy program is announced, you will keep the lead for years."

"But, Miss McGee, how can you predict such a response by the Government?" asked the baiter.

"Excuse me, James, but Miss McGee, is that the completion of your proposal?"

"It is, Mrs. Brenner, except to say that in order to keep the timing intact, I will require $10,000 within two days as retainer payment for one of the most effective lobbyists in Congress. This may also answer, in part, Mr. Albert's question."

"Ten thousand dollars?"

"Are there any more questions for Miss McGee?" There probably were but no one voiced them, Nancy thought.

"I have one then," Nancy was surprised at Mrs. Brenner's mischieveous intrusion. After all, they had been talking about this for weeks. It began when Nancy called Mrs. Brenner at her home and asked her to watch the news on chanel nine the following night. She said she would call back the next day about a possible way to double Catherine Products' sales volume. In all subsequent telephone calls, Mrs, Brenner demonstrated increasing interest and finally agreed to this presentation. Although she protested at the irregularity of the approach, Mrs. Brenner obviously saw the same apex and was merely testing Nancy's resolve. "What's in this for you?"

"Partnership in Rucker, Snells and Associates." The blunt truth seemed most appropriate to Nancy and it was to be the deciding remark.

"I should say. Well, in that case would you mind viewing our product display for a short while? Miss Simpson will direct you."

"Of course. Thank you."

No expecting father or field general experienced more anxiety than Nancy did in the next seven minutes. She tried to make herself get interested in the chronological display of products dating back to 1916. Mr. Brenner first introduced a skin lotion which he affectionately named after his first, new born daughter. What a woman, Nancy thought. Although she inherited an industry, it was her own accumen and drive that made it the leading cosmetic manufacturer in the U.S. It was during this reverie of industrial growth that Nancy was called back to the conference room.

At five that evening, Nancy returned to the office of Rucker, Snells and Associates to report the incredible events of the day. Bob reached out his hand to congratulate Nancy—which was likely the first time he touched her since the initial interview several years ago. Dean waited his turn, embraced Nancy and swung her around so violently that a sealed envelope of ten one thousand dollar bills fell from her purse.

Chapter 9

WITHIN A WEEK after the Conrad Hilton FAIR rally, the War Room membership board was busily being updated twice daily. Most of the flurry came from the Chicago area but started to affect other metropolitan areas as well. The master video tape of Dr. Wheaton's speach was reproduced and sent to Chapter Presidents in New York, D.C., Atlanta, Miami, San Fransico, L.A., San Diego, Phoenix, Detroit and Lincoln, Nebraska. The mid-west had been a rough area for membership drives all along. A respectable number of chapters were started in states like Wyoming, Nebraska, Montana and Minnesota, but membership always leveled off quicly.

The executive committee decided to devote most resources to the coastal metropolitan areas. Lincoln was an experiment to study mid-west presentation appeal. The monthly newsletter, FAIR'S FAIR, announced the more spectacualr rally activities flavored with the implication of exclusively local authorship. Chapter demands for literature, speakers and funds were becoming a diplomatic problem. Alice Trevon felt uneasy about the sudden growth indicators. She thought they needed a slower, more comfortable growth which allowed the philosophy of their movement to cure - to gain depth. Sometimes Alice even felt that FAIR was spawning a vindictive trace. It could be nothing, but, were that trace to swell and not be guided by the spirit of brotherhood which Alice so longed for, FAIR could become unfair. Alice was one of the members of the strategy committee and voiced those opinions a day earlier. Now she felt rebuffed by Connie, as if she really did not belong in the policy making arena. Alice thought herself more akin to the foreman of a machine shop. Or better, a propaganda shop. It was not so bad when the executive committe decided to do all of the rallies, but more recent attitudes indicated a power play. Alice needed some players on her side. The more she thought, the faster her heart beat. It was a matter of duty. FAIR had to remain an educator—not a demander. And that was the direction the strategy committee had taken ever since this Nancy McGee and Phil Wheaton had become involved. Alice did not even know of their backgrounds. One thing was for certain: They did not need FAIR for any physiological problems. Miss McGee was a shapely, olive skinned brunette that would turn men's heads. Dr. Wheaton was an absolute doll. A bit mature but so clean cut and powerful. In control. Apparently he was quite distinguished in his career. His voice would command attention in any discipline. Alice dreamily recalled yesterday's meeting, watching Dr. Wheaton's lips move, occasionally exposing perfect teeth. That self-demeaning description he gave of himself on TV, she thought, was misleading. He really did not have a pot belly and the attempt at balding added to his authority.

Alice wondered what Miss McGee meant to him. They arrived together but then she did not actually see them driving in together. During this introspection, she suddenly realized the subtle manipulation performed by Miss McGee. She never seemed to answer any questions but somehow the committee members volunteered answers that supported the preconcluded conclusion.

Alice was stunned during the meeting when she saw what goals and strategies were being outlined. On protest, she was reassured that this was not manipulation. Their goals were to help give people what they wanted. Ultimately such an issue would have to be voted on anyway. After all, it was a democracy and no one is about to shove something down 250,000,000 citizens' throats if they do not want it. This point was made by Flossy whose grotesque smile made the restrained hostility seem even more menacing. Alice could not figure why she experienced such alarm about FAIR. Perhaps because she had just finished her fifth cup of coffee, she decided, and prepared to leave the old German restaurant she was using as a shelter. Outside the restaurant was a Salvation Army volunteer competing with the downtown Christmas music for manifestations of the holiday spirit. Alice headed for the library down Pine Street. As she passed the Water Place Inn, she saw a parked Mercedes with Illinois tags. On a hunch, she diverted into the hotel lobby and walked up the steps to the FAIR headquarters. The automatic door closer had not enough stored energy to completely close the door to the War Room from the last person to enter. Alice took advantage of this and the newly carpeted floor. She carefully let herself in. She recalled working many nights and no one was ever there unless a meeting had been called. She heard soft talking—two women apparently. Both, fear and indignation, tormented Alice as she tried to discern the identities of her office intruders. The office door was open enough to reveal the desk's edge, a pair of lovely legs, one calmly dangling over the other, and cigarette smoke billowing from the visitor's location. Nothing was being said when Alice slowly moved closer, her legs behaving like leaden weights. The absurdity of sneaking to her own office was replaced by the explosive shock of seing five one thousand dollar bills neatly arranged, partly overlapping each other on the desk. Why not just walk in with an air of innocence and dedication, Alice reasoned.

"I'll do it," she heard Connie say. She recoiled to her previous step . . . Panic numbed her as she saw signs of the meeting coming to an end. Alice diverted all of her perceptions and muscles to carefully and promptly leaving the War Room. There was still a chance of being seen before reaching the lobby. The implications of this covert transaction had not even occured to Alice as she sped through the lobby, the revolving doors, down one block, across the library court yard and to the doors. They were locked. The lights inside were on and people still roamed about. Alice felt safe enough and turned to watch the Mercedes being entered and driven off. Two giggling school children were exiting and Alice caught the door to slip in.

Chapter 10

An order for thirty thousand pamphlets was placed with Circle Printing. They were delivered to FAIR HQ by the end of the month. The old addressograph was busily printing each pamphlet with a member's address. Five thousand extras were sent to all congressmen, key newspapers, TV and radio stations, churches and universities. Volunteers worked up to eleven hours preparing the mailings. They knew they were making history while demonstrating the process of democracy and this was the perpetuating fuel. To be a part of that communal momentum left coffee breaks forgotten. Near ten thirty, the last of the pamphlets were bundled and carried to the pickup truck downstairs. Someone delivered the payload to the post office before the mail trucks left. Others cleared the work area, brought out the snacks and called for the reserved half-keg of beer.

The party was to commemorate another giant step for FAIR. Unofficially, however, the comraderie grew from the nostalgic awareness of the end. FAIR HQ was relocating to North Michigan Avenue of downtown Chicago. The Green Bay Chapter would remain but most of its leaders would leave for the Windy City by Saturday. The Executive Director would assume the position of Green Bay Chapter President.

Alice was mostly ecstatic about this change. At least she could guide the Green Bay Chapter in the direction of understanding instead of trying to change the whole world. She was vaguely aware, however, that FAIR was rolling onto a much grander scale from which she would eventually have to withdraw. Perhaps, if she could see that the pamphlets were only catalysts, she could relax a bit, she thought. It would still take peoples' response to make such a change. If it was wrong, Congress would never respond because people would not support it. This was sufficient placebo to allow Alice to forget the meeting of the previous month, the five thousand dollars, Nancy McGee and Richard Greenwood. After all, she thought, just look at the warmth, the friendship and solidarity in this work room. Alice still hated the term War Room.

Someone turned the stereo up and switched off all but the last row of lights. The Christmas tree was still standing, but without needles. Alice plugged in the colored lights and stared at the tree. From across the room, Connie noticed Alice's shimmering eyes for a moment too long and called everyone to attention to make a toast.

*   *   *

A pamphlet addressed to Helen Davis was among the mail box bonanza laying on the kitchen counter. Helen gulped a glass of milk and nibbled a windmill cookie, sat down and prioritized the mail. She saved FAIR for last since it promised to be most interesting. A letter from her artist friend announced that he was returning to Chicago. Many municipalities had gone to black listing non-union art. His description turned from documentary to desperate. A gallery that had carried his work frequently for the past five years had just refused him. The proprietor had made a good profit off John's work but not enough to balance the scale. Apparently, a new IRS regulation provided significant tax breaks for closed-shop galleries. Although his friend at the gallery agreed that John's work was excellent and usually moved within months, he simply could not afford to give up the tax advantage. The only galleries not on the bandwagon were the junk shops. John never displayed there and was not about to start now. He promised to give Helen a call after he arrived.

Helen put the letter down and wondered how and why. John's letter sounded so passive and accepting. Why wasn't he angry, she wondered? Why wasn't he writing a letter or law suits? How could he make a living?

Helen was very worried about her friend. She knew he would not compromize by painting dictated junk. His painting was his life and he would not give it up for money. But John was not a fighter either. When something got in his way, he would more likely apologize and go another way. He never seemed upset but he certainly did nothing to disuade the systematic profaning of art. If enough people like John marshalled their forces, this could be stopped, Helen thought. Instead, the best artists seemed to be leaving the area and opening the void for the trashers. Some of the best artists were barely eaking out a living, Nearly all held some menial job. And yet, few spoke out. They just quit the Guild and moved elsewhere. Why would they not realize that when cancer is allowed to spread, soon there would be no place to move to? Helen believed that John not taking a stand was as upsetting as the trashers and manipulators who brought this whole thing about. More precicely, it was John's lack of anger that annoyed Helen. What was the use in getting upset about John, she wondered? She had her own battles to fight and win. John would have to live with his passiveness.

Helen was anxious to open the FAIR brochure. The slick, professional approach certainly did not emanate from their President. The new address meant dollars. The membership must have been growing rapidly. The mailing and the hint of forcing Congress to aid another underdog would bring more members. She tried to fantasize the inevitable momentum of growth and power. In the past ten years, the public has seen fit to provide for itself: A national TV network did a special on people leaving the high paying jobs, starting tax shelter co-ops, barter groups and other desperate attempts at making ends meet. Wealth Magazine alarmed the nation of the "Industrial Drain". Capital investments, despite increasing Security Trade Commission restrictions, were chanelled to rising third world nations. Some unions tried to seize the remaining profit mongers, as they called them, with labor contracts that gave virtual control of national industries and government monopolies to the union hierarchies. Over fifty percent of multinational corporations transfered their entire manufacturing facilities to foreign soil, leaving mostly franchised distribution centers in their wake. Unemployment was at twenty percent, a figure that earlier economists predicted would topple the system and with it, the democratic form of government. Free education through undergraduate school; free medical services for all but those earning 250% of poverty level income; free public ground transportation; and a minimum income subsidy bringing all adults to the minimum 110% of poverty level. Income tax had risen alarmingly fast until two years ago. Then all States were mandated to tax at three percent of federal level. When the "Productivity Drain" was publicised, an emergency federal tax limit of thirty-five percent was declared for all wage earned income below $30,000 per year. Many analysts thought the economy would collapse. Degreed and skilled people were leaving the country. The tax limit brought some restraint to the exodus.

By a seemingly divine stroke of insight, the Federal Reserve had prepared for these times and guaranteed all deposits up to $250,000. Their officers boasted of not a single panic. Some banks closed bown but others assumed their obligations with no major incident. Comparisons with the 1930's Great Depression had the nation in a psychological panic, if not a financial one.

Helen's first assignment back then was to research the congressional voting pattern and provide some explanatory background. Mr. Seegraph raised his eyebrows and her salary when Helen came back with a filmed, taped interview of a California Congressman who remarked: "Look, it's my job to represent people. Since fifty-seven percent of my constituency is on income subsidy, I can't hardly vote against the AMTRAN program can I?" If there was such a thing as a moment in life when one dedicates their energies to a certain mission - this was it for Helen. The cycle of more and more House and Senate votes being governed by people who for one reason or another did not produce but demanded increased consumption was vividly outlined during that assignment. That was why Helen wanted the anchorwoman job on the WRX news staff more than anything else in life. She thought she could take those events that seemed to propel her society toward collapse and give some light to the folly.

The anchor job still seemed far away but the FAIR pamphlet was to be the seed for a TV special she wanted to do. When she proposed her idea, Seegraph at first enthusiastically agreed but Harry wanted to wait. The time was not right, he felt, but had a difficult time explaining himself. "If we weren't such good friends, Harry, I'd positively hate you right now," cried Helen.

Harry laid his arm on her shoulder and asked: "can I cash in on that friendship with a one minute license to explain . . . huh?"

"Oh, all right. But that wont do much for my special." Helen pouted but knew that Harry was with her. She was more angry at herself for yelling at him.

"Maybe that's where you're having a problem. It's not just your special, you know. In fact, if you are as right as you think you are, this one belongs to a lot of thinking people."

"So?" That was Helen's signal of interest and permission to continue. "So, if you do it in the coming month, you might wake up a few people and then what?"

"Then we . . ."

"Timing, my dear. My hunch is that before this Congress retires this year, it will have been forced to act on this demand by popular pressure."

"But that's my point. We should act now."

"It's not an issue yet. A special next month would just help it to be an issue. That's why Seegraph backed off right away when I recommended it. He wont be used to make issues. We have to wait until . . ."

"Shortly before Congress votes on it."

"Well, not too close. It's got to be just right. When support is high and proponents are complacent."

"But someone else may do the story by then!"

"I'm sure they will—but not as good. You've followed this closer than anyone. Their's will be just that, a story.

You are going to provide an education."

"How am I going to do that, wise old man?"

"That, not-as-wise young woman is your job. I can't be doing everything for you."

"What I would give for a cream pie right now."

"Lemon please, if you're serious. Now, let's get back to work. You can't be rubbing shoulders with the big guys all the time." Harry departed with simulated grandeur.

"See you, your highness," completed Helen and fought laughter and tears when she noticed Harry's socks didn't match. She would use this against him at the next encounter.

CHAPTER 11

I F ONE WERE to remove money as a vehicle for communication, most governments would come to a dead stop. This one was no different. In Congress, the most difficult analytical task for anyone desiring to establish seniority was to properly balance the weight of constituent votes against the weight of dollars from other sources. The House Speaker's Office always set the pace. With experience came subtlety. Since there were so many special interest organizations, lobbyists virtually became one more 'middle man' between voters and laws. In a way, the Speaker would confide to some, it still wasn't such a bad system. With an increasing number of votes coming from the have-nots, pressure groups with significant funds were a sort of balance of power within each branch of government. The Speaker's success came from a practice of occasionally turning down some lucrative offers of dubious benefit to anyone. There was always a group somewhere, willing to pay for what most people wanted. The system still worked—it just cost a little more but then inflation has affected everything else, the Speaker noted.

When Mr. Speaker heard the cosmetic thing from Jake Vogel-Brand, he immediately liked it. Jake did not get that impression but then that was just part of the horse dealing. It would be a big job; would have tremendous effects on the budget. But, the Speaker needed a popular, new issue. His hunch told him that this FAIR group was a good enough thermometer. If he could be credited with initiating such a bill, it would take care of some of the grumbling during the last election. A lot of his own people were even saying he was getting too old for the job. Didn't have much to offer anymore. This ought to do, he decided when he called Jake back into his chambers: "Jake, my boy," as he called anyone beneath him, "I think you have a good idea here. The problem is, no one has ever brought it up. PUW hasn't even discussed this one. It would be like starting from scratch. That takes a lot of valuable time and friends if you get my meaning, my boy." The Speaker was looking directly at Jake and he rarely looked directly at anything.

"I think I do, sir and I'm prepared to compensate for such resources." "Good . . . good. But why the hurry ? These things take time, you know. It has to be drawn up, go through committees, over to the Senate and then the toughest of all, the Pres. He's really been on my ass lately to cut the biggies. All the old fool ever talks about. And it's not an election year you know. If you could just wait until next February, it would be much better."

"I'm sure it would, sir. But as you must know, I'm representing a client who is very sensitive about involvement. It was a take it or leave it proposal with no negotiation possible. So, I'm afraid we will have to succeed by November." Jake was getting a little worried. He knew he would be held up for a sizeable sum but really wondered himself if anyone could achieve results so quickly.

"I see. I see. Hmm . . . To test the earnestness of your client, it would be helpful if the National Democratic Party somehow found a $100,000 donation in their receipt."

"I understand, sir. Is that all for now?"

"Yes. But I'm afraid it is only the begining. Is your client solvent enough to see this thing through?"

"That depends on you, sir."

"Yes, I see . . . Well, I expect it might take up to a million to get it to the White House."

"And then?"

"And then we'll have to see where the public is. After all, this is a democracy."

"I thank you for your time."

"Good day, my boy, good day."

Jake went to phone his client. Nancy agreed to meet him in Pittsburg at two in the morning at the AMTRAN station. The Pennsilvania, Ltd.

would allow enough sleep so she could fly back to Chicago in time to prepare for and meet with Mrs. Brenner.

O'Hare Hyatt was chosen as a suitable place for lunch, away from the office and the local crowd. Mrs. Brenner was uncomfortable with the idea of being seen in the company of Miss McGee. Not a flinch, waver or tone change was perceptible to Nancy after her request of a one million, twohundred thousand dollar deposit in escrow. Mrs. Brenner agreed but felt it was more appropriate to have an account that Nancy could draw on. All moneys would go to a bogus company from which Nancy, its Treasurer, could draw. No single withdrawls were to exceed twenty-thousand dollars. Mrs. Brenner reiterated that if legislation did not follow in time for a Christmas promotion, the Rucker & Snells deal was off.

Nancy returned to her office looking like the victor of a traffic jam. More likely, she was its victim because Dean Rucker and Bob Snells had left the office and she wanted to discuss an idea she had. Nancy thought about her goal, November, the partnership. It all was begining to look possible and already did not seem like enough anymore.

* * *

The FAIR staff barely had time to move in to their new national headquarters. The mail came in two full bags daily from the terminal annex. Back in Green Bay, Connie Ballew would always go through the mail herself when she was there. Over twenty volunteers had already responded from the Chicago City Center Chapter, so she picked a leader type and gave her the mail to sort. All preprinted return address envelopes were to go to Connie. The rest could be opened and processed.

When the mail volume exceeded three bags, Connie Ballew called an executive meeting for no other purpose than to wallow in their success. The Membership VP had to commute from Green Bay but she and her husband were making plans to relocate. At the meeting it was voted to change the by-laws to allow for a modest salary for the FAIR officers and increases for Tom Stuart and the new Executive Director. Tom would work out the details.

In the pamphlet sent two weeks earlier, one of the tear-out pages for members included space for new members recruited, requests for membership forms and a check off box to indicate if they had sent the tear-out card to their congressman. By last count, over five thousand had responded with entries in all three blanks. The bow was drawn. The arrow was aimed. This analogy was suggested by the Secretary/ Treasurer who liked to see herself quoted in the meeting minutes. As for the five thousand dollars, Connie never quite found the right time to mention it.

CHAPTER 12

T HE LETTERS KEPT coming, memberships swelled to the point of requiring a data procession firm. They automated the tracking of members and prospective members for mailing demographic statistics and projections. FAIR's growth was spurred by the band waggon effect. The newer the converts, the more zealous they were. And more powerful. Some presumed conservatives turned out to give their support.

Older people, in general, were inordinately supportive. A spokeswoman for the Grey Tigers described the sad state of affairs senior citizens were relegated to. Many, she said, were still young at heart but felt confined by their wrinkles and other geriatric problems.

The entire orchestra of support and demands channeled through the FAIR organization exposed a frantic pursuit of the lost or denied fountain of youth. The Congressmen who withheld their support were called the harbingers of antisocial villainy. Newspaper editorials and TV talk shows were taken over by the idea of cosmetic equality. Once the proponent views were sufficiently repeated, the air became saturated with attacks against opponents like vigilante gattling guns. Respected careers were indiscriminantly blemished in the fever of what had truly become a national debate.

Dr. Wheaton took a leave of absence from his research organization to satisfy the hungry audiences from coast to coast. Since his original statement at the Chicago rally had apparently been the spark to this ideological contest, the media—and therefore the public—considered him the most authentic spokesman for cosmetic equality.

The demand was clear; an absolutely unprecedented number of letters and telegrams were received by Senators and Representatives. There was a dispute over Committee agenda readjustment to include the Cosmetic Equality Act proposal in time. The House vote was scheduled for September. Meanwhile, the Supreme Court ruled in favor of the House Ways and Means Committee to include the Cosmetic Equality Act proposal in the Committee agenda. All that remained were some unconvinced, stubborn Congressmen whose constituency did not yet support the Cosmetic Equality Act.

*   *   *

Nathan Tyler was appointed the new FAIR National Executive Director. With all the available data, it was easy for Nathan to zero in on the problem areas. It was the old fashioned Midwest, he would suggest to his volunteer friend. The FAIR members in those areas would have to be mobilized. In this final contest, psychological guerrilla warfare was called for. Nathan questioned his friend frequently about this when she was at the HQ. She usually did not offer much in response. She seemed to be more concerned that he had coffee and prompt typing.

Nathan concluded that she was not political or idealistic but simply enjoyed being around the action when she could. She usually came in the mornings. When she did not show up, he missed her. He would look to the door frequently or scan the work area for that familiar reddish afro. One day when she was there, he hid his anxiety and finally asked: "Miss Davis, do you have a moment, please?" He addressed everyone by their last names unless he was alone with them.

"Certainly, sir," Helen patronized, "did you need something?"

"Well, yes, actually. Would you have time to talk over a glass of wine or lunch?"

"Why, I suppose so. Is anything the matter?"

"No, of course not. We don't even have to talk about FAIR. In an hour, maybe?"

"Fine," said Helen, puzzled by the formality, and returned to her compiling. She wondered if he was attracted to her or if it was something less complicated but more awkward. He was not a bad fellow. Quite good looking, actually. About thirty. What confused Helen was his absolute devotion to the task and technique without apparent ideological comments or concerns.

"Thanks for coming with me."

"You're welcome. So, tell me about you. Where are you from?"

"I was going to ask that about you. Isn't that funny?"

Helen blushed since there was not anything funny and she lost her words. Finally: "What did you do before you got here?"

"Lots of things. Worked in a print shop. Drove trucks. Tried the Marines for a while."

"Sounds well rounded. You've obviously had a stint in academia."

"Some. B.A. in English Lit and a Masters in Business Administration."

"Aha!"

"Why, what . . . ?"

"I couldn't decide what background you were coming from. Now I see . . . Are you a red neck?" This was accompanied with a teasing smile.

"No."

"Aren't all Marines?"

"Most, I suppose. At least then. It was just a good way for me to drift for a while and still eat. Couldn't get a job to save my life. So, I joined in hopes they would pick my spirits up . . ."

"Did they?"

"Na. Tried to smash them some, actually. Once they found out about my formal education, I was a marked man. If you stuck out in any way, someone would push you back. Even meanness had to be average. Just one big happy machine. I almost forgot I had an education. Anyway, I learned to blend in and when I got out, I used the G. I. Bill to get a Masters in Business."

"Really sounds interesting. Sorry for calling you a red neck."

"It's OK. I'm not. Anyway, what do you do when you're not serving the cause?" There was a touch of cynisism in this question. Helen noticed and was prepared for the question.

"I work in the WRX-TV commissary as a waitress."

"I'll bet you meet some interesting people there."

"Well, I see them, but they rarely have time to chat."

"I suppose . . . May I have lunch there sometime?"

The: "No," came out a little louder than Helen had intended and she, hopefully, compensated with, "you have to have an ID card or visitor's pass. Besides, with the crazy traffic, it would take you an hour for transportation."

"I get the feeling you wouldn't want me to. Maybe I was being too forward?"

"No, not really. I . . . just would rather you didn't see me as a waitress but as a volunteer. It's more glamorous."

"Well, popular it is," Nathan welcomed the change of subject, "I still can't believe the response. People are usually so apathetic."

"I guess it's what people really want, huh?"

"Sure is, and it's exciting to me to see Congress responding to what people want. Don't see that everyday."

"You think it'll pass in September?"

"It's bound to. Who stops an avalanche?"

The bottom of the mountain, Helen thought but decided not to voice it. Instead: "I suppose you're right." A long silence sent them both on different thoughts. Helen tried to picture him as a Marine. And as a truck driver.

Actually, all that fit better than his present niche. He certainly had the talent for managing the avalanche but not the temperament. He was calm, self-assured and introspective. Except when he was around Helen. This was the first time she saw the starch out of his collar. He should have looked more like that raving, trash peddling artist who announced the Guild Union. But he didn't.

Nathan's reverie did not reach such analytical heights. He tried to fantasize her breasts without encumberments. He thought about her hair—which he did not like. He remembered her graceful walk. Not at all like a waitress. For her, walking wasn't work. Her body was more like a means to elegantly move her head from one place to another in a straight line. Nathan realized that he had been staring at Helen all this time. An offer for another glass of wine seemed an appropriate way to break the silence. The remaining conversation was not able to recapture the previous mood. Some alien feelings wedged their way between the two. For different reasons, Nathan and Helen were anxious to bring their meeting to an end.

*   *   *

The congressional fight for the golden egg was on. The House Ways and Means Committee had to determine which committee would determine which department or agency would absorb the new responsibility of administering the Cosmetic Equality Act and absorb its likely immense budget.

The variety of contestants defied rationale. Among them were the Departments of Commerce, Labor, Productivity, Understanding and Wellbeing, Housing and Urban Development, the Interstate Commerce Commission, Social Wellbeing Administration, National Science Foundation and the Office of Equal Opportunity.

The Office of Intergovernmental Relations and the Office of Administrative Procedures Agency braced themselves for the equivalent of a national emergency. For one week of Congressional debates, no other laws were passed. Some editorial fiscal consciences cited that the Congressional void was the most effective austerity measure of recent years. Ultimately, the Department of Productivity Understanding and Wellbeing was chosen as the appropriate gaining organization with provisions for involving other areas when their expertice and existing resources warranted such distribution.

". . . and that's the news tonight for the Chicago area. Please stay tuned for an editorial special on the controversial Cosmetic Equality Act proposal. This has been Roger Morton for WRX-TV."

There were no regular sponsors for the special. Possible FCC retribution to sponsors' regular programs and short notice left the station to finance its own program as a public service production. No small effort was required by Seegraph to earn approval from the board.

And thus it began: "Good evening, Ladies and Gentletrien. I am Winston Seegraph, Production Manager for WRX-TV, and I am very proud to introduce this program. As you can imagine, a televised presentation requires a tremendous amount of research, preparation, editing and a myriad of other activities. Most of the people involved are never seen on the screen. The following program was prepared by a young lady named Helen Wells who will also present this important special—'Cosmetic Equality Act: Yes or No?' We invite your opinions by writing to: CEA Special, WRX-TV, Post Office Box X, Chicago, Illinois, six-zero-six-zero-one. A sample of the responses will be aired this time next week. And now, Miss Wells."

Helen was sitting at home in self-imposed isolation, watching the pre-recorded special. The introduction by Seegraph was a special surprise to her for the open support it brought with it. As she saw her own image, she felt the first stab of self-consciousness by what she was about to hear again. "Equality is a dangerous myth. Synonymous use of the phrase, 'equality' and 'equal rights', has guided our nation to philosophical bankruptcy. While equal rights remains as one of our society's most important goals, equality is an unrealizable negation of nature. That we would consider, let alone use, valuable monetary resources and congressional energy to create and support a Cosmetic Equality Act illustrates how close to defying nature we stand as a nation. Tonight, I want to present to you the views of four distinguished scholars that might generate a re-thinking of the Cosmetic Equality Act among some of you."

"Never has our country been so rapidly overcome by a new concept. But, then perhaps the groundwork has been laid long ago. Originally, the now well known FAIR organization started in response to what its creators considered unfair hiring practices by a restaurant owner. By last winter, a FAIR spokesman, Dr. Wheaton, introduced an expansion of their goals when he challenged our Government to take care of the outside as well as the inside of its citizens. By now, this lateral excursion from the main theme, 'We're All The Same Inside', has become the primary frontier. In less than a month from today, the diligent efforts of FAIR INCORPORATED may result in taking money from every taxpayer to provide cosmetic services for allegedly unattractive citizens. My guests on this program all openly oppose passage of the Cosmetic Equality Act. Questions to them will be geared to exposing the long-range implications of such an act, an area which few have seen fit to expound upon."

"First, I would like to introduce Dr. Lawrence Abels, Professor of Economics at our University of Chicago. Dr. Abels is the author of two widely quoted books, numerous articles for professional journals and special economic advisor to the President during the Viet Nam era. I might add that his advice was ignored in that capacity. Dr. Abels, where is our economy going?"

"Thank you, Miss Wells. In my opinion, to use the jargon of our younger set, down the tubes. In relation to other currencies, our dollar is still quite sound. But, in a discussion of trends, it is a gloomy picture, indeed."

"But we have a healthy Gross National Product. Someone must be doing quite well."

"That's true, but the numbers are decreasing. The Government has permitted and encouraged a concentration of wealth while giving a show of fighting the same through their antitrust and security control activities. When this country was started, of necessity, hard work was most amply rewarded, partly with survival. By the advent of the industrial revolution, ideas brought the greatest reward because their impact was farther reaching than manual labor and the means of production and implementation of ideas were there. The latest trend of greatest reward per the amount of energy invested is becoming non-productivity. Increasing revenue is being diverted to the maintenance of non-productive elements of our society. One element that has been with us a long time is war and more recently, some space exploration. The justification of these activities is subject to argument for the survival of our nation. The resulting technological advances are of benefit but would likely have come of their own when a return of capital investment seemed promising to certain industries. I mean to discuss the effects of spending funds with little or no hope of any kind of return. The element I have been most interested in studying is the effects of supporting nonproductive people in our society. I don't want to appear indifferent to the fate of people who are ill, unemployed, preoccupied with crime, etcetera. However, when there is a real limit to what can be done for this element, an analytical look is required. I tend to look at problems in terms of returns. X amount of social program dollars need to bring Y amount of return. If we increase X without restraint, we arrive at a margin of diminishing returns. For example, if we spend thirty thousand dollars to rehabilitate a criminal, in the long run, that person may return to productive society and, instead of consumimg more tax dollars in police, court and prison costs, may pay taxes and return our investment. We most likely prevent a certain amount of crime by providing a limited amount of welfare. However, if we invest a greater amount of funds on welfare, say three X, then the incentive to get back to productivity is decreased, and we are unlikely to get our investment back. In fact, one might say the crime then falls on the Government for expropriating more funds than what was required for stability. At this point, of course, we have to decide what we expect our Government to do—provide a minimum or a maximum amount of stability. I certainly don't expect the standard of living of welfare recipients or prisoners to be as high as those productively employed. It's not even a moral issue; in the long run, it simply doesn't work."

"You've answered several more questions I had ready. We talk about government doing this or that. As large as it is, could you point more specifically?"

"Yes. Ideally, of course, one would have to say that the voters, through Congress and their President, could have what they wanted. Many voters want precisely some of what we now have. Even if a majority wanted different, we would have to look at the internal workings of Congress. There is a tremendous built-in resistance to certain change which does add some stability. One thing Congress generally does not deal with is federal regulatory agencies. These agencies have developed an immunity to control much greater than other areas of government.

We then have to go no farther than our Federal Reserve System. It has the power to bolster or wreck havok with our economic system. The administrators are not accountable to the citizens and most wouldn't know what criteria to judge them by anyway. There have been situations in the past where the Reserve Board Chairman couldn't be contacted by telephone, and we nearly bankrupted our economic system within one day. Such a concentration of power seems ludicrous in a democratic nation. The Reserve System has performed some important stabilizing actions, but the overall effort is inappropriate at the federal level. Through their judgement and decisions rests the health of our entire economy. When there is such a specific area of government controlling the amount of money available, we can see that therein lies a source of inflation. Inflation is the most subtle enemy. People will revolt at an overburdening tax structure, but inflation is more difficult to fight or even recognize. Going back to the depression of the thirties, the primary cause was too much money made available by the banks through the support of the Federal Government. The economy overheated until its emptiness was exposed. Many suffered, but others became wealthy. This event probably would not have occured without centralized cooperation. Independent banks would have turned loans down or have folded for their own lack of sound judgement. But the entire system would not have folded. What we have now is a more cautious board of governors. The inflation is slower and the recessions are smaller and not too destructive. But, the power to heat up or cool off the economy is there and goes virtually unchecked.

Then, beside the slow robbing of our worker's purchasing power, there is another potential crime of catastrophic nature. When deficit spending benefits the few and the power to control money supply rests with a few, the potential for collusion and corruption and the greatest crime of the century since the last contrived war lies just around the corner.

The Cosmetic Equality Act doesn't compare to that magnitude, of course, at least not in the short run. In my opinion, the Cosmetic Equality Act is just one little crime that could be perpetrated by many who fail to look at the long range effects. One reason the passage of this Act is so important to me is that it reflects the most blatant disregard of no returned investment—unless, of course, you are in the business of manufacturing cosmetic products."

"Your comments were so inclusive that I have only one more question for you. Dr. Abels, what advice would you give the average citizen, the layman who is not a professor of economics?"

"Ecomonics needn't be such a complex subject. It can be reduced to a personal checking account. The amount of income depends on how much money one actually earns by creating and selling products or services. If one spends beyond that and relies on credit, one must be aware that tomorrow's productivity will not all be available for spending if the current debt is to be repaid or just the interest maintained. All the economist does is try to unweave the complicated web of implications. A dollar spent on defense, housing, rebate, etcetera, all have far reaching, compounding effects. If we are to make the proper decisions of taxation and spending, we need to understand all of the implications. Unfortunately, much effort goes to clouding the implications with attention focused on immediate rewards. For the interested layman, I would offer this: Every time your Government takes a dollar from a worker and gives it to someone else, you need to consider two things. One, is there likely to be a proper return of investment? And two, is some specific industry or group of people likely to make a substantial gain."

"Dr. Abels, I thank you very much for your insight and I am sorry we don't have more time."

"Thank you."

"Next, I want to welcome Mr. Jeremia Zeus. Mr. Zeus is an anthropologist originally from Sheffield, England.

He has been involved in so many other disciplines that anthropologist seems too restrictive a description of his talents. He described himself earlier as being too busy trying to figure out the world to take employment seriously. Mr. Zeus, how do you get away with it and is that really your name?"

"A sizable inheritance, modest living and a huge ego answers your first question. Purely contrived to spare embarrassment for my family, the second."

"I see. Please give us your thoughts on why the Cosmetic Equality Act has earned a serious following and the effects it might have on our social fabric."

"Love to. I notice you deal in groups of questions. That's interesting. I can prepare for the second while discussing the first . . . Our advance in technology has not been matched by an advance in philosophy. One result is that our increasing number of people, somewhat alienated by a lack of ability to understand or control their system, have a tremendous need to be pacified by images. The legal constitutional system of government has been undercut by an army of lawyers who worship the letter of the law rather than its intent, legal images instead of justice. For some decades, the creativeness of the entertainment business and related industries were sufficient.

Once desensitised in that manner, the next step was for people to demand some of the action. Examples are: Cut rate tour packages visiting seven major cities in a week, continued adult education of dubious value, adrogeny and flamboyance in clothing styles. In themselves, these are not necessarily undesirable. It is the lack of depth that symptomizes an illness of the spirit. Americans—and the rest of the western world—have become a very impatient lot reminding me of a group of toddlers screaming: 'I want it NOW!' More immediate satisfaction is necessary. Imagery is the latest pasttime; it delivers the goods NOW. Purchased doctorate degrees, get-rich- quick schemes, cosmetic surgery, salvation for the price of standing up and walking forward; they're all on the increase. Charisma is more important in heroic figures than deeds and values, knowledge, essence, ability or accomplishment. Religion, politics, education, music, even life styles themselves, have been reformed by the demand for charisma. Once our heroes have succumbed to this demand for mediocrity, the masses must next have it for themselves. If everyone is to look like they're living the beautiful life, they of course, must look beautiful. In fact, I suspect in the long run, that a cosmetic equality program could become more important than the once controversial medicare/medicaide programs. In summary, it will become more urgent to look good than to physically, mentally and spritually feel good—the all-American short cut to happiness."

"You seem to be implying that the origin of this proposed ACT, the FAIR Organization, had little to do with the popularity of the Cosmetic Equality Act."

"I'll more than imply it. I will state it. FAIR is nothing more than a catalyst and not a very sophisticated one at that. How they hoodwinked your Congress into responding is impressive to me, but the massive demands for affirmation of the Cosmetic Equality Act comes from a very ready public that FAIR was lucky enough to stumble upon."

"Then you don't put much faith into educational programs like this one to cause a significant change?"

"Courageous question, Miss Wells. Frankly, I think the most we will do is go on record as opposing this nonsense and for that I must commend you and your broadcast organization. However, to have significant impact in this matter, you would have to undo generations of conditioning and outright lying, be more effective than all the psychologists over the century and more dazzling than all the advertising industry."

Helen thought of John, her artist friend and realized he never called, and she had been too busy to write. She was sure he too thought her efforts were futile, but he would never say so. "In my naivete, I'll hold on to my hopes. Have you had time to think about the second question?"

"Yes, I have . . . The long range effects of the Cosmetic Equality Act itself is probably self defeating. I envision some futuristic society where everyone looks the same and subsequently, looks become totally pointless. We'll simply move on to some other theatre of inequality and destroy it—if the stage remains standing. The important projection to make is what is the long range effect of the social attitude that favors a Cosmetic Equality Act. The answer is simple: Our demise. The only living organism that approaches equality is the single cell called amoeba. From there, the more complex the organism, the more unequal each one becomes from its fellow. The homosapien has in excess of ten thousand traits in his genetic pool. By random combination through sexual reproduction, we produce an inexhausitble variety of fellow beings. When we introduce environmental reality into this diversity of beings, we get inequality. Some are better able to survive than others.

To wish it otherwise may be noble but unreal. While in the short run, some of our friends may die because of this inequality, in the long run, it confirms our success as a species. Adaptability to change originated from the worst of a species not being able to survive and thereby leaving a stronger gene pool. The moment we help the unalterably weak to survive and reproduce, we are opposing the natural order of things. The idea is as futile as the other extreme of Adolf Hitler's ludicrous concept of a master race by extinguishing an inferior race per his description. There is some flexibility, as must be since we cannot ignore values and culture. To give someone a shot of penicillin to fight off VD is only a minor infraction on nature. Besides, the victim may have learned something in the process.

When we maintain, through modern medical miracle, someone's precarious life so he or she can propagate further unhealthy offspring, the insult to nature is greater but perhaps still bearable. When we provide food to sustain an entire society bent on copulating itself out of existence, we have further interrupted the lessons of environmental demand. The fact remains and always will be with us no matter how noble our sentiments: There is a limit to how much insult our total earth system will absorb before it vomits the offending species from its nurturing sphere. There is also a limit to how much any subsystem, such as our society, will absorb. The answers aren't easy. There is an envelope of flexibility. We are not about to let someone starve to death before our eyes because he broke his back and can't work for a year. The fact that he worked before and that he will probably work again has earned him our temporary support. On the other hand, we don't purchase a fifty thousand dollar home for a divorced woman with several children because she needs a favorable environment for her offspring—at leaset not with tax money. We perform that abomination through the modern slave trade called divorce settlement.

For a stable but not too stable society, the answers lie somewhere between starvation and the fifty thousand dollar home. Even some animal societies provide temporary help to its troubled members. For human beings, the most successful society is one that provides enough stability to encourage risk taking and simultaneously leaves enough instability where successful risk taking is rewarded; where the outcome of each act is not totally predictable. The moment you attempt to guarantee survival, happiness, attractiveness, success and all the other parameters that, in nature, are not guaranteed, you aim at the demise of a species. To artificially elevate the weak members of a group to the strong, initially weakens the integrity of the group and ultimately dissolves the cohesiveness of cooperation. The idea of cosmetic equality, I suspect, will become a problem not so much in the biological as the social strength of our group. At least, that is what will tend to destroy us first. It is particularly interesting to me to note that the same people who have so diligently worked to assist nature in fighting industrial pollution seem quite in favor of human pollution."

"If I may summarize your answer, you are saying that an attempt at cosmetic equality will ultimately decrease the cooperation level of our society."

"Precisely. And when cooperation decreases, the only remaining vehicle for continued cohesiveness is force. In my opinion, the passage of the Cosmetic Equality Act will move us closer to a police state, and I don't think I am overstating my projection."

"Mr. Zeus, I thank you for appearing on our special and hope you are ready for the response to your comments which we will undoubtedly be forwarding to you."

"Ah, yes. Always the fan mail. I'm quite ready. Thank you for inviting me."

"Our third guest is Professor Marian Lindstrom, probably best known for her inflamatory comments in a weekly, syndicated column carried by most of the major newspapers around the nation. Professor Lindstrom is a Political Scientist and Philosopher by education and avocation. She has been active and vocal in this area for thirty some years. Professor, welcome to our program and would you please start by talking about what kind of system you think we have that would foster the passage of a Cosmetic Equality Act?"

"Thank you, Miss Wells. Let me begin by talking of labels; of calling it what it is or isn't. Capitalism or communism. It's not capitalism. It's not socialism. It's not fascism. We really don't know what it is anymore.

There are no lasting values in use. The Government won't admit to half of what they do until a generation later. Government employment, government expenditure and government influence is increasing. We seem to float on a sea of expediency with no guiding philosophy. We no longer subscribe to any of the - isms; we supposedly don't do enough for the non-productive; we take too much from the productive, and we lie about either. We point to the atrocities of unchecked capitalism and concentrated powers while ignoring the fact that Government has made most of the concentration possible. We berate socialism as a foreign philosophy and move closer to it with every session of Congress. We arm a mighty defense orgaaization to protect us from the very countries we send food, money and technology to. We engage in a contrived battle between labor and business as if one were possible without the other. The real war is between the producers and the takers. That places business, labor and minimum gavernment on one side and excessive government, needless welfare, thieves and dishonest and polluting productivity on the other. We are a nation of fence sitters. In the long run, our workers will grow tired, our engineers, scientists and technology will belong to other nations or cartels. Our GNP will drop, our strength be diversified and used up throughout the world. We will be a nation of has-beens with nothing more to offer or protect than a symmetric network of hamburger and chicken stands. Theonly national structure in history to attempt an experiment with recognizing desirable human rights will be - if it hasn't already - abondoned for a secure, grey mediocrity. The Cosmetic Equality Act is but one more inevitable step to total government control. With the gigantic and growing national debt, our nation is more controlled by the concentrated money powers who are not accountable to the public or any branch of government.

The public doesn't even know for the most part, who the national debt is owed to. International banks, insurance companies and large holding corporations, that's who. Each program we approve without the funds to back it up makes us more indebt to these money lenders as well as destroying the purchasing power of our workers' dollars. Although the international commerce is at the highest level of cooperation in history, making war unlikely, the gigantic money lenders are forced to seek military parity between major world powers to insure their loans are paid back. Every indicator shows power and freedom leaving our citizens and migrating to multinational establishments who then divert their funds to other nations engaged in robbing the citizens of their freedoms and natural resources."

"You sound totally pessimistic and somewhat angry. What would cause a turnaround of this trend?"

"Nothing. There will be no turn around. While our Government has little inclination and power to return freedom to its people, it is the people themselves, in increasing numbers, falling prey to the trend of something for nothing and urging our Government for more. Only the people could cause a turn around, and it would probably require a revolution of some sort. Certainly a thinking revolution. A value revolution. Our shoddy television programming alone will deter that from happening. At any rate, for a century, we have increased our dependence on cheap, foreign raw materials to elevate our standard of living. To maintain this flow of raw materials at rapidly rising costs, the giant multinational corporations have developed—by our indirect demand—a world wide allegience to their obvious advantage and thereby greatly weakened the national concept. Slowly, the control of our commerce and industry is migrating to foreign or supra-American control. Americans are selling their economic souls for raw materials."

"Then what is happening is not out of line with the democratic process?"

"No. Neither is a majority electing a dictator. But both are processes that show no respect for a philosophy of individual rights."

"Isn't that the right of a democracy?"

"No! Not a constitutional democracy. We wouldn't allow a referendum vote to legalize killing all Rh negative blood type people. Even if eighty percent voted yes on such an issue. Because that goes against a basic philosophy of individual rights,"

"What then is wrong with our process, in your opinion?"

"Never before have we had so many voters asking for—demanding—other peoples money simply because they need it."

"Do you suggest not letting non-productive people vote?"

"No. That would be wrong and dangerous. The only solution is to abide by a constitution that protects individual rights to property and productivity. Then no amount of legal pressure could allow the unchecked robbery presently implemented by our income taxes."

"What do you label this world wide trend?"

"The void of our non-philosophy is being filled by a very definite socialism arriving ultimately at international fascism."

"Do you think people will condone this trend?"

"Socialism is working in many countries with no massive exodus of people. I'm sure some depict their system more accurately in their public schools than some of the fictions we feed to our unwary youngsters."

"Doesn't that give socialism some credibility?"

"Yes. It exists along with dictatorships, tribal rule and religious governments, and they all work to some extent.

Fear, expediency and superstition have ruled for millenia and will probably continue. Their only source of credibility from an individual rights standpoint is that 'might makes right'. My point here remains that we need to attach the correct labels to our governments so citizens will know which philosophy is removing their freedoms and fruits of labor."

"Couldn't you come up with a name for our present system?"

"If you insist. At this time, we are at Expedienism oozing disrespectfully toward socialism and the hell beyond."

"Then you infer capitalism no longer exists?"

"Only as subsystems where it is expedient to allow it to exist."

"Expediency means making things work. Are you opposed to that?"

"Such a question. Does the end justify the means? The choice is - do we make it work a certain way come hell or high water or do we make it work restrained by a philosophy of individual rights?"

"We are still basically a Judeo-Christian nation. Isn't that a restraining philosophy?"

"Where have you seen more unrestrained bloody violence than in religious clashes? I'm not demeaning the virtues of voluntary Christianity, although they haven't been practiced much during the past nineteen hundred years. I'm talking about Christianity, Judaism, Islam or any other religion becoming civil law. When you have a nation of Judeo-Christian socialists putting restraints on capitalism, you get exactly what you've got: A mixed up non-philosophy that ultimately succeeds in creating a vast mediocrity where grey will be the mandatory color."

"Don't you think the Republican and Democratic Parties provide a philosophical balance for each other?"

"Yes, but look at what they are balancing. The Republicans are somewhat willing to give capitalism a chance although in a much corrupted form. But they do want to control morality. The Democrats are quite willing to be liberal in the control of morality as long as they can collectively control and distribute the material wealth.

Neither exercises the value of individual rights. Both advocate the violation of individual rights, sacrificing them for collective wellbeing. Both camps operate in the Cartesian separation of mind and matter. Any line drawn between these two camps will never intersect the line of individual rights. A choice between establishment Republican and Democratic Parties is like a choice between electrocution and brainwashing for an innocent victim. We make much ado about the choice when the real choices between freedom and incarceration are never mentioned."

"I'm afraid we are running out of time already, but would you make a final statement on how we would deal with the demise of non-subsidized, non-productive people as their ignored corpora litter our sidewalks."

"The supposed humanists who encourage institution upon institution to ensure the equality and survival of unequals with someone else's productivity obviously have the lowest esteem of human nature while claiming to have the highest. They imply that without these institutions, nothing would be done. I doubt that the bodies of the needy would litter the sidewalks. Too many times have I seen human compassion assemble its resources to volunteer help to disaster victims or friends helping each other on a smaller scale. Local aid programs are supported in increasing numbers in spite of extravagant Government taxation. But such programs of voluntary help have their limits as does human compassion. The basic requisite is that the needy person do all he or she can to help themselves. Voluntary help never goes to the point of guaranteeing a standard of living equal to the community average or exceeding that of the helper's. The services guaranteed by the CEA are so far removed from the voluntary gifts of human compassion, I can only say our system has become absurd to even consider it.

H. L. Menchen once said: 'Democracy is the dictatorship of the booboisie. He wasn't speaking of constitutional democracy. He was describing what is happening now."

"Thank you very much, Professor Lindstrom. That certainly answers my opening question."

"Thank you for the opportunity. It was a pleasant change."

"Unfortunately we have very little time for our fourth and last guest, Dr. Ronald Holtz. Dr. Holtz is the pastor of the Valley Baptist Church of Cleveland Ohio. We thank you for travelling to Chicago for this interview and appologize for our poor time management."

"I appreciate the opportunity and I'll get right in to the national topic. What I have to say will be quite short and it may not make sense if you are not coming from my perspective."

"And what specifically is that perspective ?"

"Well, obviously I am a Christian. This means I have accepted Jesus Christ as my personal saviour. And for the benefits that come with his sacrifice there are some obligations. I am obligated to advance the Kingdom of God.

Which means putting all else in second, third or last place. It doesn't mean I don't have fun or enjoy the many things this world has to offer but it has it's proper place in my list of priorities. Cosmetic equality is so far near the bottom of that list that I haven't had much time to worry about it. I have no problem with cosmetics or even cosmetic surgery as long as it has it's proper place. Obviously, if someone has some major disfiguration it is a more important issue than if you have misplaced your tube of lip stick. No one can say where the proper priority for cosmetic issues should be for any given person nor can we judge where someone has placed that priority in their personal scheme. What I do know is that when we tax people to pay for someone elses cosmetic needs, it does not seem to be what Christ had in mind. He did say we should render onto Caesar what belongs to Caesar but he did not elucidate on what belongs to Caesar. When we reflect on were our relationship is with God, an easy tool is to think of the one thing that we think we can not live without. Whatever we come up with, that is our greatest danger of a false god. If we think that how we appear physically to others is one of the most important things in our lives—and I suspect that is the case for many—then we have some priority problems because that does not serve God and that line of thinking does not lead to happiness no matter how much of the federal coughers we rob to try and make it so. That's really all I have to say and judging by the man pointing to the clock, you have managed the time perfectly."

"Thank you Dr. Holtz for being so understanding. Well, Ladies and Gentlemen, that concludes the scholastic portion of our presentation, and we invite your written responses. I want to conclude this special with an observation of my own marked by my truly sad silence. Some time ago, I happened to attend an artists guild meeting with a friend. What started as an attempt to guarantee the acceptance of artistic trash has resulted in the unionization of artists. At first, public institutions supposedly owned by you, refused to display non-union art.

There was no public outrage. A subsequent tax preference was given to private galleries displaying only union art. Then union executives began to demand not only outrageous dues but restrictions in painting style. Last week, I attended an art exhibition at a private gallery. You will now see the silent coup de grace of American contemporary art. Good night and thank you for being with us."

The TV screen then displayed a slow panning of fourty some paintings apparently done by an artist who favored reddish hues with an imaginary light source usually from somewhere above. The video camera retraced its path at close-up range to reveal the names of over thirty different artists.

*   *   *

There were no fence sitters among those viewers that gave a written response including some newspaper editorials. Much of the condemnation was general, but a significant number of responses criticized the stacked deck of panelists trying to cover too many issues. This, Helen expected. There was one telegram however that fit neither category—or both: MS. DAVIS WELLS, CONGRATULATIONS ON YOUR THOROUGHNESS AND YOUR REAL HAIR. Signed NATHAN TYLER.

VOLUME II

Chapter 1

A STRAW VOTE indicated the Senate would pass the CEA if the House voted two thirds in favor. The FAIR Executive Committee decided one last push was appropriate. They had enough support for a national demonstration. In practice to oppose FAIR was considered lacking in intellectual sophistication. Most universities and colleges had a campus chapter of FAIR supporters. Before adjourning for summer break, campus members of FAIR were asked to check in with the nearest local FAIR Chapters for possible developments. This request made it possible later that summer to mobilize the restless members in time for a demonstration even though the House vote was to be moved up nearly one month. Nathan arranged a blanket contract with a charter bus company. If a minimum of twenty-five people left from any one location, the fare to Washington, D.C. would be discounted ten percent. On top of that, Connie agreed to release sufficient funds to further discount another ten percent for all members who submitted their reservations by August. Nathan ordered a mailing to announce the demonstration through all local chapters. A press release announced the proposed demonstration with anticipated attendance of fifty thousand. At Nathan's suggestion, the executive committee drafted a letter to be sent to all Congressmen, reminding them of their duty to represent the will of the people. To give credit for such responsible discharge of duty, the voting record would be reproduced in the next FAIR'S FAIR newsletter which had a circulation of over five million.

The thought of hundreds of congressmen receiving these letters caused Nathan to experience the most exhilarating feeling of power he had ever known. His spasmodic laughter occasionally drowned out the rush hour traffic. Nathan felt compelled to go to the place of his only rendezvous with Helen. He had done that often in the past months. It helped him to keep his task in perspective. Seeing Helen host her special left him bewildered, angry, doubtful but longing to see her again. She seemed so passively secure when they were together; so unconcerned with anything above just keeping busy. The afro wig should have tipped him off. Nathan prided himself on being an excellent judge of character. The same trait was most responsible for his uneasy feeling with the executive committee President, Connie Ballew. He resented Connie Ballew the most. She seemed to take extra care in subtly reminding him of his place in the organization. The rest were just drifting along with events. He also wondered why he never heard about their original executive director.

It was Helen who heard from Alice. A letter finally found its way through the studio's elaborate mail system. With all the responses to the special, Alice's letter marked PERSONAL remained in a miscellaneous file basket for a week. When Helen read down to the signature, followed by President of the Green Bay Chapter of FAIR Incorporated, a response was certain. Alice had requested a meeting in Milwaukee. The letter was sent two weeks ago, right after the special. Helen made immediate and repeated attempts to call her. Never an answer. On her way out, she tried to call once more from the lobby. On the ninth ring, an out-of-breath voice answered: "Hello."

"Hi. This is Helen Wells from WRX-TV. Is this Miss Trevon?"

"Oh, yes. It's Alice, please. I assumed you didn't respond because of all the mail you must get."

"No, normally, I get very little mail. Yours was accidentally delayed. What's up?"

Alice told her.

CHAPTER 2

THE CEA DEMONSTRATION was an explosive success. News coverage prior to the event caused an avalanche of response. People that did not even belong to FAIR attended in the thousands. A week before the demonstration, a few maverick newspapers and broadcasters picked up on the term DOG IN. By the day of the demonstration, the thirty-five thousand participants affectionately adopted the term themselves. The most common news clip to illustrate the demonstration was of a speaker/celebrity at the demonstration when she said: 'The people have spoken. Let the Government respond. This was Wanda Rainier, a plain looking but ample breasted activist film star of recent renown. Her rags to riches journey made her a favorite daughter of popular opinion. Post news coverage declared the August DOG IN would probably go down in history books. This was correct.

The CEA was passed within the month by the House and the Senate. The nation waited for the formality of the President's signature. His participation and support was passive thus far but the Press Secretary assured his captive audience that the President would make an announcement of his thoughts on the CEA at the proper time. That time had arrived. The cameras were set in the press room. One close up revealed ten pens to be used in making the signature. It was August thirty-first, ten in the morning. Attendance was expectedly low for such an anti-climactic event. It was now the President's time to speak. He was a seasoned man, unemotional during conflict and hard to disuade. As he entered the room, someone said: "Ladies and Gentlemen, the President." All rose until he was seated. He picked up the document presumed to be the Act, took the first pen and studied the document. His face was flushed and severe. He rose, not looking up, "Ladies and Gentlemen . . ." his arm suddenly made a stabbing jesture as he buried the pen's point in the document. The pen broke. The President's hand started bleeding. ". . . Ladies and Gentlemen," he shouted, "this . . . this abomination of governmental process, this Act, is pure excrement. To say anymore would demean my office. Good day." As he turned to leave, he swiped the document to the floor. One reporter had enough composure to plead, "Mr. President . . .", but his effort went unrewarded. The door from the press room slammed shut.

*   *   *

The concept of national response is usually reserved for declarations of war, energy crises and assassinations of presidents. The inexplicable behavior of the President once again put the nation's components in a united state of shock. The next day words like insane, unprecedented, undignified, impeachment, political suicide and conspiracy were the common diet of all editorial comment. A majority of the public was furious.

Helen Wells and perhaps several million were ecstatic, awed and worried about their President. Congress immediately organized to override the veto. The actual process was academic since over three-fourths of Congress had already supported passage of the CEA.

*   *   *

On September seventeenth, the CEA was law. Nine months were allowed for implementation. This timing would coincide well with the next fiscal budget. Meanwhile, one hundred twenty-five million dollars were earmarked for designing and setting up the necessary programs, manpower and facilities.

The contest for a new PUW Assistant Secretary to head the Cosmetic Equality Agency was obscured in red tape and not news worthy. "The public would have to settle for crimes of lesser dimensions for a while," Helen mused as she reviewed news copy of post CEA fame. Helen's printing office friend in Washington, D.C. thought she might want to know the recommended candidates for the highest postitions in the new CEA. She also described the formation of a recommending agency called the National Institute of Cosmetic Health. It was to be tasked with performing research related to cosmetic health. There was only one name that has been proposed so far for its Director although there was no decision yet. The candidate was a Dr. Philip Wheaton. Rumor had it that the House Speaker recommended him highly and he will probably be appointed. After the call, Helen demanded a portion of Harry's time to piece the next special together. Then she read the Federal Register containing the Cosmetic Equality Act :

Public Law 101-596 103rd Congress, S. 9857 September 17, 1984

Cosmetic Equality Act of 1984

AN ACT TO ASSURE EQUAL OPPORTUNITY IN THE PURSUIT OF HAPPINESS, AS IT MAY BE CONSTRAINED BY COSMETIC INEQUALITY, FOR EVERY CITIZEN; BY ASSISTING AND ENCOURAGING THE STATES IN THEIR EFFORTS TO ASSURE COSMETIC EQUALITY; BY PROVIDING FOR RESEARCH, INFORMATION, EDUCATION, AND TRAINING IN THE FIELD OF COSMETIC ADJUSTMENTS; AND FOR OTHER PURPOSES.

Be it enacted by the Senate and House of Representatives of the United States of America in Congress assembled, That this Act may be cited as the "Cosmetic Equality Act of 1984"

CONGRESSIONAL FINDINGS AND PURPOSE

SEC.(2) The Congress finds that the pursuit of happiness is constrained for some citizens when afflicted with undesirable cosmetic appearances, and such afflication reduces the optimum utilization of our human resources through decreased motivation,

(b) The Congress declares it to be its purpose and policy, through the exercise of its powers to assure, in as much as possible, the cosmetic equality of its citizens,

(1) by authorizing the Secretary of the Department of Productivity Understanding and Wellbeing to set standards for the equitable distribution of benefits authorized by this Act,

(2) by providing research in the field of Cosmetic Adjustments including psychological factors involved; and by developing innovative methods, techniques and approaches for dealing with Cosmetic Adjustment problems,

(3) by establishing causal connections between prenatal diet, genetic influences, birth techniques, childhood diseases and undesirable cosmetic appearance,

(4) by providing training programs to increase the number and competence of personnel engaged in the field of Cosmetic Adjustments,

(5) by providing for the development and promulgation of Cosmetic Equality standards,

(6) by encouraging States to assume the fullest responsibility for the administration and enforcement of their Cosmetic Equality Act laws by providing grants to the States to assist in identifying their needs and responsibilities in the area of Cosmetic Equality, to develop plans in accordance with the provisions of this Act, to improve the administration and enforcement of State Cosmetic Equality laws, and to conduct experiments and demonstration projects in connection therewith,

(7) by providing for appropriate reporting procedures with respect to Cosmetic Equality, which procedures will help achieve the object of this Act and accurately describe the nature of the Cosmetic Equality problem,

(8) by establishing joint industry/commerce and citizen efforts to reduce Cosmetic Inequality arising out of congenital or environmental disturbances.

DEFINITIONS SEC. (J) For the purpose of this Act—

(a) The term "Secretary" means the Secretary of the Department of Productivity Understanding and Wellbeing.

(b) The term "Commission" means the Cosmetic Equality Review Commission established under this Act.

(c) The term "Cosmetic" means all factors relating to the outward appearance of a person.

(d) The term "Committee" means the National Advisory Connnittee of Cosmetic Equality.

(e) The term "Director" means the Director of the National Institute of Cosmetic Equality.

(f) The term "Institute" means the National Institute of Cosmetic Equality.

(g) The term "Assistant Secretary" means the Director of the Cosmetic Equality Agency. ect.

Chapter 3

THE CEA MOUNTED an aggressive recruitment and hiring program. Initially, about fifteen hundred people were required at all GS levels. The newly created jobs and favorable citizen response brought all significant opposition and grumbling to a halt in most media channels.

The major task was to design the criteria system. Allotments would have to be fairly and efficiently made. One of the frequent objections during committee debates was not philosophical but administrative. It was argued that administration costs would be nearly equal to the allocated funds for cosmetic services. There was no way to get around evaluating each applicant at least once to determine the appropriate level of benefits. It was hoped that one total evaluation per person would be sufficient. Changes over time, cheating, age limits and renewable clauses had to be dealt with. A moderate sized administrative machine was inevitable to the policy task group members.

*   *   *

Nathan Tyler resigned from FAIR to assume the position of Regional CEA Director of the Great Lakes Region. Nathan was the youngest to be appointed regional director. He had made an excellent impression on the Assistant Secretary, Dr. Jacob Masteson, as well as the interview board. Nathan could not contain his joy at being selected. He had to share his success by celebrating—but the only appropriate partner was

Helen. The WRX-TV switchboard operator assured him that Miss Wells would return his call. Counter to his prediction, she did.

"Hi, Nathan. How have you been?"

"Busy, successful, happy . . . and lonely."

"How can that be with all those dedicated people bustling around you daily?"

"Well, that's what I called about. I resigned."

"You did? Oh, Nathan, that's really great! What brought you to your senses?"

The advisability of this call faded for Nathan. He thought of changing the subject but she probably would not believe him anyway. "I'd like for you to help me celebrate my new job."

"Oh ! Well, what's it going to be?"

"Let me preface by asking that we respect each other as people although we seem to be philosophically opposed."

"I'm not sure if I can separate people from what they do . . ." Helen paused long enough to decide if she should end the whole thing right then. ". . . or if I want to." If it had been anyone else, she might have hung up by then.

There was something of a little boy in Nathan that she liked. Curiosity was beyond control. "Tell me about your new job."

"I've been appointed Regional CEA Director for this area." Nathan held his breath and tried to remember if he just said this as an announcement or a question.

"Oh my gosh . . . and you want me to help celebrate? Do you realize that your boss will be my arch enemy? Do you know what that makes you?"

"I . . . I guess . . . that makes me one notch below your arch enemy . . . so it could be worse? Look, we're not going to contaminate each other. I need to talk with you." The desperation of insecurity reflected in the word 'need' settled his request into a comfortable proposal for Helen.

"How do you plan to celebrate?"

"On top of the John Hancock for dinner."

"Hope you don't fall off . . . Must be quite a salary . . . OK, I'll meet you there at eight."

"Why don't I pick you up?"

"Because I have to make sure I don't get contaminated. I'll meet you."

It was not quite what he wanted but more than he expected. To minimize the risk of loosing ground, he just said, "Thank you. See you at eight."

It was a chilly, windy Tuesday evening in Chicago. Parking was scarce. The walk was bitterly cold. Nathan cursed the slush that found its way into his shoe. The elevator took too long even though his ears were popping from the rapid ascent. It was already five to eight. He exited on the ninety-fifth floor, straining to see a familiar face. He became aware of his desperation and it made him feel scared. It was as if he had to have a pardon or a blessing from Helen before he could allow himself to feel good about his new position, or anything. Yet, Helen seemed the most unlikely person to give him that blessing. So why, he wondered, was he exposing himself?

Sure, he had reservations about the CEA. But he also had the same reservations on other national policies and wars. The point was, and this was his bastion of defense, that the CEA was the result of the democratic process if anything ever was. It was the people's will. Whatever points Helen's TV Special guests made could not undermine that fact. The CEA is the majority's wish. Rarely has there been such national unity on one issue. To ignore such unity of purpose would certainly be a flagrant violation of the government serving the people.

Of course, it would have its costs. There are always costs to caring. Aid to parentless children costs too, and no one gives that much objection." Maybe Helen is already in the waiting area. Nathan hoped she was not. Just to be able to deliver her to a table would imply some aquiesence. He was ready for anything but total rejection.

"Have you been helped, sir."

"No, I'm waiting for a Miss Wells. She hasn't arrived yet, has she? I have a reservation."

"And the name, please?"

"Tyler."

"Yes, eight o' clock. Did you say you're dining with Miss Wells?"

"Ah, yes, I did. I mean, I am." He tried to remember if he chose this place or if Helen did.

"Splendid. Your table is ready. This is Miss Wells' favorite table."

"Her . . . favorite table . . . Thank you."

"You're welcome. I'll show her in when she arrives. A cocktail waitress will be with you in a moment."

"Thank you."

Nathan's mind reverted to a non-productive introspection while watching the traffic on Michigan Avenue below.

"Favorite table, my ass," he mumbled. "Next, the dinner will be on the house. This goddamn tie is choking me."

"Are you talking to yourself already, Nathan? That usually doesn't come until after ten years in government service."

"Oh, hi!" Nathan shouted as he stood up, nearly at attention. The curtain kept his tipped chair from falling and hopefully from being noticed. Chivalry returned in time for him to pull Helen's chair out and help her get seated.

"Thank you. And you're looking fine. I'm used to seeing you in corduroy pants and field jacket."

"Yea, well I'm trying to create a new image." Everything he thought, said or did seemed to come off flat.

"Is that your starting statement?"

"Give me a chance. Let's order first. It may be my last objective decision tonight."

"Come now. You can't be scared of your old personal secretary."

"I'm not. I'm scared of a crusading newscaster."

"Which of us is devoting sixty hours per week to a cause?"

"Wait. We're starting all wrong."

"You're right. I guess I'm not completely sure why I'm here and it shows."

Nathan was relieved to hear some ambivalence. "I just needed to talk with you."

"Just talk, eh?"

"Yes, just talk. It doesn't even matter what about—just so you're talking."

"Why? This is like a meeting between Stalin and Solshenitzin."

"Maybe they did."

"Why would they?"

"They're people just like us."

"Bullshit. Stalin was a monster just like you'll become."

"So I'm not a monster yet. That's a relief. I really want to talk about this but not fight, OK?"

"OK. Tell me why it's so important to talk to me. I think I'd rather go back to being a sex object with a wig than a mind object."

"You were never a sex object."

"Oh come now. Didn't you love it when I catered to your every executive need like a dumb broad should?"

. "Why are you so hard?"

"Nathan, I hate what you stand for. I hated wearing that wig and doing your crap work. Or at least, I thought I should. I always looked forward to being near you until I remembered what you were doing. I'm hostile because I don't like feeling confused. And I only said feeling because my thinking isn't confused at all. I'm annoyed because I don't know why I'm here—what you want from me. Being hard compensates for my insecurities. Does that explain it sufficiently?"

"Yea, it does . . . I don't know what to do with it."

"If you can tell me why you need to talk to me. Me of all people. I'll devote all my spare time to zapping your organization. I'll find your weak spots. I'll figure out how to make you look ridiculous. Watch what you say to me even now because it will all be used against you."

"Against me or the CEA?"

"Against . . . both. You are the CEA."

"Then maybe I was wrong. I thought you might be for me but against the CEA and that's why you are the one person I need to talk to."

"You mean you're not sure of what you're doing?"

"For being intellectually superior you sure are slow on some conclusions."

"Well . . . not really. I must have known that much or at least felt it or I wouldn't have agreed to have dinner with you."

"Now can we order?"

"Yes."

"I couldn't have eaten if we couldn't get past the first hurdle. Let's make a truce. I know there will be times where we won't be able to share information. But when we do, let's make it the truth, OK?"

"Think you can handle it?"

"I don't know . . . I have to. You have something I don't have. Maybe I can learn. I know you're honest in your convictions but so am I. Both of our convictions have a price. Who is to say which is the best?"

"Every human with dignity and intelligence."

"True, but they won't always agree, will they?"

"OK. I suppose unless I claim infallibility, I'll feel compelled to go along with you on that."

"That's what I needed to . . ."

"But don't think for a moment that I didn't mean what I said. I'll use the media to ridicule the CEA, to embarrass you, to indict the public that supports this farce."

"OK. But you won't hit me will you?"

Helen emitted one spasmodic laugh, momentary silence, then burst into a fit of laughter. The dinner was a good idea.

CHAPTER 4

THE NORMALLY PLEASANT walk down Lincoln Park Avenue was interrupted by obstructions and jack hammering. A half block was barricaded against pedestrian traffic so a sign could be safely erected to its permanent height. Elegant manuscript type, green letters on black background spelled out THE McGEE IMAGE. The name reminded Helen of Alice's story. She asked a workman what business it would be. Some kind of advertising agency was his answer.

When she arrived at the studio Helen had a thought on a future information investment. She gave Alice a call at the Brown County Court House in Green Bay. Alice offered a depressed, "Hello."

"Hi, this is Helen."

"Oh, hi. How's your battle going?"

"Slow. I need your help again."

"At your service. This job is so boring and it's only eight thirty."

"Then I caught you at the right time. How would you like a different job? Better paying; lots of people; travel; glamor; should I go on?"

"Go on, go on."

"Would you be interested in working for the CEA?"

"The CEA? I think you know my answer. Why are you asking? I've heard all their recruiting advertisements, but I just couldn't. Not after what I've seen."

"Why not?"

"No. It's all so crazy. I feel guilty enough for having started this whole silly mess. If I could only erase that day."

"I can't say that I agree with your original motives, but that was long ago and now it's out of your hands . . . but you could help to oppose the CEA."

"By working for them?"

"Yes. And keeping me informed."

"Isn't that illegal?"

"So was the American Revolution. The CEA is not the CIA. There's nothing secret so it's not illegal. Perhaps improper in their eyes but not illegal."

"You want me to be a spy?"

"Well, I never thought of it that way, but if that makes it more glamorous I guess that sort of fits."

"It seems dishonest or something."

"How do you think the free press functions?"

"I suppose but . . . but the CEA isn't really corruption. I mean it is all out in the open, isn't it?"

"I don't know, but I always have to assume it isn't. There is only one way to find out. Are you game?"

"I need to think about it. I don't know if I'm the type for all this intrigue."

"That's why you're precisely the right person. Besides, it should be quite interesting. You can find out first hand how your government works to serve its people."

"I don't know," missing the innuendo, "it feels funny."

"I don't want to pressure you too much and I appreciate your sensitivity. Take some time to decide."

"OK. I'll call you back in a couple of days?"

"Fine."

"Thanks for calling. I don't think I'll be bored the rest of the day."

"Good. I'll wait for your call. Bye, Alice."

"Bye, Helen."

Alice's heart was pounding as she contemplated her new life. She did not realize she had already made up her mind to apply for a CEA position until she found herself across the road at the Post Office during her lunch break. She picked up a civil service application form.

*   *   *

Helen always went through her mail before the activity onslaught by one o'clock. There were frequent surprises but none to match a note from the Chief Editor of the Chicago Herald:

Dear Ms. Wells :

If you have the time and inclination to talk about a weekly column, please give me a call.
I shall reserve thirty minutes to discuss at three thirty tomorrow afternoon.

Sincerely, Robert North

The note was hand delivered. She let it dissolve in her mind for a while.

Harry had to be consulted first. She knocked on his open door.

"Good morning, Miss Wells."

"Miss Wells? Expecting me?"

"I've been expecting you."

What is this?"

"Didn't you get my message?"

"Ahm, no. I guess I haven't finished my mail yet. What's up?"

"You are."

"What does that mean?"

"It means our anchor man has announced his resignation for personal reasons, effective February fifteenth and you are being considered to replace him."

"Harry, you sweetheart." Helen lept over his desk to give Harry a hug.

"Ahem. Is that anyway to behave toward a superior?"

"Yes!"

"That's what we like about you. To the point."

"Who is we?"

"Never mind."

94

"When is 'we' going to decide?"

"In about one minute. I'm waiting for a phone call."

"In a minute. I don't believe this . . . So how come you're not with them trying to sell me?"

"And be accused of pushing my prodigy? In the long run, it's better this way."

"Why has no one said anything?"

"They just found out last night. And in case you turn it down, they'll need time and there are only fifteen days left."

"Turn it down? . . . Why did he resign?"

"Getting divorced. Apparently a messy affair."

"I'm glad for the opportunity but that's a shame. I like him. That's why I never talked about his job to anyone but you . . . Why me, Harry?"

"For lots of reasons. But there are some other excellent people being considered. I think it was the special. You projected the image they wanted. Especially when you give a hard time to people you agree with."

"It's not an image."

"I know and that's what makes you a strong candidate. But on the job, everyone's an image."

"Actually, I came to ask your opinion or maybe even permission on something else. Bob North has asked me to do a weekly column. What do you think? My head is spinning."

The phone rang. Helen froze. Harry answered, "Yes . . . Yes she is . . . It's for you." Harry kept a serious straight face.

"This is Helen . . . Yes, sir . . . Oh, yes . . . I'll be right up . . . Thank you . . . Harry, I got it," she screamed. Harry put both hands, wrists crossed, over his face for protection.

That night, Helen decided it was her turn to celebrate. And of course, there was no better candidate for the honor of sharing this celebration than the new Regional CEA Director. Over a bottle of Chateau Lafite—Rothchild, she could offer Nathan a chance to surrender before she launched her daily battle of TV news commentary and weekly columned barrage of acid words. What would she do, she mused, while dialing his number if he said 'no' ?

CHAPTER 5

A LICE CALLED HELEN six days after the last call to report she had been chosen for an immediate clerical opening in Green Bay. They were setting up some kind of field office. Helen congratulated her and said success must be in the air. She recommended that Alice wait a month and then apply for a position in Milwaukee. Meanwhile, she should sometimes work overtime without asking for pay, speak in dedicated CEA jargon and assume other forms of the ideal employee. Helen recommended that Alice write to Nathan Tyler and tell him that she preceded his position in FAIR but did not like the executive committee. In fact, he hated the executive committee, especially Connie. Helen sounded like a mischievous little girl and both of them giggled. She completely forgot to tell Alice about her own promotion.

Helen kept her interview appointment with Bob North of the Chicago Herald. North was understanding of her predicament and agreed to keep the offer open until the end of February. She really wanted the column. It reached so many people. If it turned out well, it might even be syndicated. A note to Helen from the Government Printing Office described some difficulties in appointing Dr. Wheaton. There was turmoil between the House Speaker and several Senators during the confirmation hearings. The President's input had been conspicuously missing. She wrote back and asked her friend to check it out.

Helen gave Nathan a call and asked if he would meet her for lunch. He cautiously agreed. Their conversation at lunch went like this: "Hi," Helen started.

"Is this a social chat, or will you try to turn me into an informant?"

"Would you like to be one?"

"No." This answer lacked the humor and the easy going warmth Helen was used to.

"Is anything wrong, Nat?"

"No, not really."

"Remember our contract." She stared straight into his eyes.

"Alright. I'm uptight about being with you where people can see us. They might not understand."

"What could be more natural than the heads of state and press to engage in professional conversation?" This was to cover her rising anger.

"I know, I know. But publicly, you are opposing me."

"And privately, too," Helen interrupted, "I'm opposed to your function. Not you."

"Yes, but . . . it doesn't look right. I mean, people don't separate our personal feelings from our professional stands."

"Look who's talking. You asked me to separate the two when you were appointed and now you tell me it's impossible!"

"Helen, don't yell, please. People are staring at us. Couldn't we meet at night? Some place more private? That's all I want."

"So, I'm not good enough to be seen with during the day, huh? Bye, Nathan. I think I'll have lunch with someone who isn't ashamed of me."

Nathan never looked up. Helen walked out, delighted at appearing like a wench and embarrassing him. After she left, Nathan startled the waitress when he pounded the table and coarsely whispered, "Damn."

Helen could not decide if Nathan's discomfort came from him or from what was expected of him. It was unlikely that he would admit to pressure against fraternizing with the enemy. The pressure probably was there. She did decide that Nathan was in over his head. He really was too young to be reporting to the assistant secretary of a Federal Regulatory Agency. Too naive. He would never be able to handle the occasional compromises of integrity and the continuous exposure to nonsense inherent to the job. How hard would they have to push him, Helen wondered, before his real nature surfaced? With someone dedicated like Nathan, it would only be a matter of time before the conflict emerged. Until then, he would undoubtedly struggle desperately to not listen to a timeless part of his mind.

Actually, what Helen wanted to know from Nathan during the non-lunch was the amount of the budget that had been committed. The next day, a Printing Office letter preceded the public news by two days to announce the President had impounded the CEA funds. That sort of answered Helen's question.

An outraged Congress demanded Supreme Court intervention. Ultimately, the Court would rule by eight to one that to impound funds of a reasonable magnitude for the execution of an Act of Congress was unconstitutional. Quite predictable, Helen thought.

"Two days," Helen screamed into Harry's head.

"What's the punch line?"

"Harry! That is the punch line. It was delayed TWO days."

"You have more than the CEA to cover." In one week, it's your show."

"I know. I won't be lopsided. You'll see. We have an excellent staff and it's not just my show."

"Just wanted to remind you."

"We're not going to stop being friends, are we Harry?"

These were questions that Harry found difficult to contain within the framework of corporate protocol. He would only give her a tiny portion of the total reservoir of love and encouragement available. "Helen, I'll be there, watching. Just like always . . . OK?"

"Thank you . . ." Helen put her head down, trying to contain the compassion and fear. It was a gesture of accepting the burden of coming times.

CHAPTER 6

S EVERAL DAYS FOLLOWING the Supreme Court ruling to reinstate all originally appropriated CEA funds, the President's Press Secretary announced a News Conference to be held February fifteenth. The Conference would be preceded by the State of the Union Message. The entire session would be from the White House Press Room instead of the House of Representatives. Such an affront to Congress would not go unrevenged.

WRX-TV was prepared to make the network broadcast of the Presidential messages. Helen was getting ready for her anchorwoman debute. The President's message was to provide an excellent opportunity for local comment. She planned an informal discussion with the other newsmen in the last five minutes of the ten o'clock news.

During the six o'clock news, Helen introduced herself as if she naturally belonged at the anchor seat. This was precisely how she felt. There was plenty of news to distract viewers from the novelty of a new anchorperson. A longshoremen strike was tying up commerce on the east coast. A 747 passenger jet crashed on take off when a small single engine craft attempted to land head on without clearance. The three flight officers were killed with no other injuries. American supplies, reinforcement steel and concrete were discovered used in a Cuban sponsored hospital in South Africa. The State Department investigator was fired for disclosing his discovery. Etcetera.

The faithful viewers accepted Helen's professional, authoritative demeanor, were happy to see breasts and hair with the news and patiently waited for sports and the weather.

The ten o'clock news was to be a repeat with only minor juggling to allow five minutes of commentary. For this, Helen prepared dilligently. She covered her opinions with Harry. These consisted of a primary theme: The State of the Union Message was a non-message. However, minutes before going on the air, the WRX-TV staff was informed that its national affiliate, VEC, was the only national network that did not develop technical problems during the thirty minute, live Presidential Message. WRX viewers first discovered this and Helen's flexibility during the commentary. The commentary was more of a questionary: What were the odds of two major television networks accidentally blanking out a White House conference and a State of the Union Message? What were the reasons behind it? It would have been unwise to engage in anything but questions that evening.

The next days provided some answers. United Broadcasting Corporation was served an injunction to cease operations immediately. WRX-TV as well as hundreds of other local affiliates were left in a panic to provide all of their own programming. Millions in advertising dollars were about to be lost. As quickly as the injunction was served, it was withdrawn. UBC resumed normal broadcasting. FBI agents infested the United Broadcast Building in New York but offered no operational interference. UBC President, Max Kohler was already on his way to meet with the Attorney General to plead relief.

Helen was asked to refrain from commenting on this matter until the dust settled. Similar requests were made to all affiliates. Although she understood and empathized with the network's sensitive problem, Helen had little patience with lack of candor. She promptly went to Bob North to accept the offer of the weekly column.

* * *

The McGEE IMAGE office was now functional. A handsome, male secretary surrounded by various shades of green coordinates was the main attraction for passerbyes. Helen only noticed him to the extent that she never saw the possible proprietor. The young man seemed more intent on being noticed than progressing in his work.

She decided to have a better look.

"Good morning. And how can we help you?"

"Good morning," cheerfully ignoring his standard, cheerful greeting. Helen looked around as if she considered purchasing the office. "You could introduce me to the other that makes you a we."

He looked confused. His red ears announced his embarrassment though he did not know why he was. He closed the pages to an obviously important document. "You mean Miz McGee, then?"

"Perhaps. Is she in?"

"Not yet. She is expected by ten thirty. Would you like an appointment with her?"

"Who is she expected by?" Helen enjoyed teasing this average version of Gentlemen's Quarterly latest recommendations.

"I expect her!" GQ said this as if expecting a reward for solving the puzzle. Helen fantasized a new equation for a dumb blonde.

"That must start her day properly. Before I commit to a meeting, can you tell me if you specialize or accept contracts of a general nature?"

"Well, both actually. Miz McGee would be ecstatic to describe our services."

"Ecstatic, huh?" This she had to see. "All right. May I meet with her tomorrow at one thirty?"

"Let me check . . . Ah, yes. She is free then. May I say who she will be meeting with?"

"Good heavens, young man! You don't know? . . . Til tomorrow."

Helen spiraled out of her seat, past the fern and out the door. After twenty-five feet of sidewalk, she turned a corner, let out a scream and leaned against the wall with uncontrollable laughter. Upon resumption of her composure, she imagined GQ trying to cope with his sudden void.

CHAPTER 7

LUFTHANSA FLIGHT 137, a half full stretch Boeing 707, made a smooth stop at Philadelphia International. "Oh, danks be to Gott im Himmel," mumbled the passenger in seat fifteen A. Blood returned to her fingers as she released her grip of the arm rests. Instructions in French, German and English introduced the passengers to Philadelphia, gave a small weather report, asked them to remain seated for their own comfort and thanked them for flying Lufthansa.

Finally, the craft was ready for deplaning. The aisles instantaneously filled with people. A few cheated by standing early. Johanna Baumberger remained seated. She was still sensitive to being stared at; especially among strangers. Her heart began pounding faster and flushed her left cheek with warmth. She instinctively reached up to cover her right cheek. Whenever she became excited, this cheek felt like it leaked fluid.

Ms. Baumberger was met at the airport by her sister. Their twenty years separation came to an end with hugging, kissing, crying, tissue and broken English. Ingrid was one of the few people with whom Johanna did not feel self- conscious. Nothing had changed. It would be good to have such a friend again. They both went speechless and shook their heads as if in disbelief of past memories and miseries.

"Ver ist Josef?"

"He's on night shift this week. So now he's sleeping. I told him I wanted to be alone with you for a while anyway."

Johanna burst out in more tears. The sobbing made her apology inaudible. "Oh Gott in Hinnnel, I am zo happy to be here. Such a lonely place in Ebersberg."

"Stop crying now. You won't be lonely again. And Josef was always fond of you too. You'll like it here, you'll see."

"I am already liking it. I can not help crying."

"Let's go in here." Ingrid took Johanna's hand and led her into the coffee shop. They chattered about lost friends and relatives. Sometimes in English and other times in German they quickly reaffirmed their common youth.

Before leaving for the deserted baggage area, Ingrid pulled a book from her purse. She slid it across the table while Johanna blew her nose. Ingrid then leaned back and relished in the reflection of red, moist eyes as they slowly lowered, read the title and looked back up with tenderness. She ran her fingers down the dust jacket as if it were delicately embossed leather. THE HISTORY OF THE UNITED STATES OF AMERICA.

* * *

"Miz McGee, your client is here. Shall I show her in?"

"Of course."

"Miz McGee will see you now."

"Thank you." Helen thought of adding, 'you're so kind,' but focused on the entrepeneur instead.

"Good afternoon." Nancy saw a vaguely familiar face but no name.

"Hi. I'm Helen Wells. How are you?" . . . Who are you? What are you doing here?

"Fine, thank you. Geremy didn't say the purpose of your visit."

If Gentlemen's Quarterly Geremy's last name was Quentin or something, Helen would have to think of something serious to keep from laughing again. "Well. I walk by your new office every day. Quite charming, incidentally."

"Thank you."

"For a start, would you explain the range of your services?"

"Certainly. We offer virtually any type of service associated with media image. This covers anything from people to products related to improving one's image."

"How fortunate . . ." Helen tried to remember all the cautions that Harry implanted in her head. From Alice's information, this was the same Nancy McGee. ". . . Then you may be just what I need. I've contracted to do a weekly column for the Chicago Herald. I want it to be successful enough to make syndication a possibility. Would your firm be interested in such a task?"

"I think so. Can you give me the nature of this column?"

"Yes. I intend to use it as a social critic." Helen looked for some response but found none beside words.

"What restraints are you under from the editor?"

"Good taste—nothing more at least so far."

"It sounds very interesting. I must be candid with you. We are a new firm and I have limited experience in professional imagery. Most of my previous work has been in product image. I feel, however, that most of the concepts can be applied in the same manner, successfully."

"As long as I have the final word on all output, I'm willing to risk your lack of experience. There are other factors to consider in success. In fact, you might say I'm struggling against the same restrictions as you."

"That's really true." . . . Nancy was still just recovering from the unsolicited fish she had on her line. ". . . Well, can you provide me with some preliminary information: Your background, goals, what image you want to project."

"I'd like to try something different. Would you be willing to work up a proposal without that information and see what you come up with? Under such constraints, of course, I would be willing to pay a fee for the proposal."

"I can't refuse such a challenge."

"It's agreed then?"

"Yes, I'll have something for you in a week. I do need a set of photos. Do you have some available?"

"Coincidentally, yes. I'll have them sent over today."

"Great." Nancy rose. "Thank you for your confidence and have a good day, Miss Wells."

"Good bye."

CHAPTER 8

HELEN HAD JUST answered her fifth phone call in succession when the button for her third line began to blink again.

"OK. Thanks for calling . . . Bye . . . Yes?" Her manner was less than inviting for casual conversation.

"Helen?"

"Yes, yes. Can I help you?"

"Hi. This is Nathan."

"Oh, hi. I'm sorry. They're driving me nuts today." Then she remembered she was angry with him. "What do you want from me?"

The last words felt cold but Nathan was determined to remove the last meeting from his—and her—memory.

"Your opinion. You must have seen Alice Trevon once or twice back when the trial was on. What do you think of her?"

"Why . . . and why ask me?"

"Because I trust your judgement," and he quickly added, "on some things. I received an application from her for the Milwaukee office. By next week, I have to pick five provisional area directors and assistants. Seems like she would make a good candidate."

"Nathan, don't try to involve me in your empire. Why did you really call?"

"I . . . I am trying to do a conscientious job. Do you find fault with that too?"

"It depends . . . OK, I've seen her a couple of times. She would fit in well in my opinion. However, also in my opinion, anyone who fits in well with your empire doesn't rate well with me."

"Let's not go into that now . . . Please. Administratively, you do think she would work out?"

"She has the qualities of a good manager. Does that eliminate her from the competition?"

Nathan got as far as, "Why, of course . . ." before he realized the tug on his leg.

"Let's keep this clear. I'm speaking of her apparent qualities as a manager. I am not recommending anyone for CEA work."

"That's all I really wanted."

"You sure?"

"Well, I . . ."

"What, Nathan?"

"I thank you for your advice."

"Forget it. I have to go now."

"Oh! Of course . . . See you."

"Bye."

*   *   *

Both involved networks denied complicity in any attempt to sabotage coverage of the State of the Union Message. Both agreed to broadcast a video tape, borrowed through the courtesy of UBC, to demonstrate their good faith. The anticipated threat of broadcast license revocation never came for UBC. Business went back to normal. Except, the President of the United States knew. White House operations were back to normal as long as he ignored the CEA issue. No laws had clearly been violated. Disagree as he might, Congress and the Supreme Court had properly moved to check his opposition to CEA. Perhaps he was wrong to oppose such a popular demand. If only his wife were still alive. Someone he could trust for sure. His Press Secretary seemed loyal. His friends in the House and Senate were aloof—maybe scared. He was scared. No information from him was secure. There was no way to communicate with the rest of the world without interference—or at least without surveillance. There were allies out there. Outside of the White House walls. Newspaper clippings had a new column in the Chicago Herald by a Helen Wells. Her name came up once before in a summary report. This time he gave no indication of interest, but he had to communicate with her. She must be of extraordinary courage, the President thought. The column was certain to offend the FBI and FCC chiefs. He followed her column for three more weeks and decided she was of kindred spirit. He wrote a letter using presidential stationary, folded it inside a blank page and inserted the combination into a blank envelope. On the outside, he put Ms. Helen Wells' TV studio address with no return address. An avalanche of anger tumbled and grew in his mind.

*   *   *

WRX President, Mel Harper, had posed the question of Helen's column to the Board. He wanted their open approval now while she could still withdraw without much notice. An anchorperson writing a column was without precedent. In a half year, he reasoned, if a conflict of interest question was raised, it would be too late. He could foresee problems, especially from the FCC. He had not confronted Helen with any further restraints. Nor did he feel the need to. Her common sense was already demonstrated, but her power would increase. In a year or two, any independent station would pick her up . . . and Mel did not want to lose her. She was a perfect demonstration of his corporation's intent not to be controlled by popular whim. Now was the time to give her support.

The board of directors, at the advice of the Chairman, put the question to the best judgement of each member. He moved for resolution at the next board meeting. Helen had authored six columns by then, a limited investment. Nielsen ratings indicated that WRX-TV news had gone from thirty-six to fourty percent of the viewing audience. Since she anchored the porgram. there were no signs of jealousy from other news or staff members. She freely gave them credit for their performance on and off the air.

Bob North said the Chicago Herald circulation jumped five percent at Helen's first column. He also said that her ad agency contributed significantly with radio spots, newspaper ads and about five, well placed bill board ads. The two on Kennedy Freeway alone were seen by a third of the Chicago area's reading population. To the best of Harper's assessment, everyone involved some way with Helen Wells felt good about their contribution and association. It was a little puzzling to Harper that not a single column ever mentioned the CEA. Perhaps it was some more of her common sense showing through. He secretly hoped for some action in that arena, but the deal was to not interfere.

* * *

Nancy McGee got an angry phone call.

"What in the hell possessed you to have that Wells broad for a client?"

"She asked me to do a campaign for her. She pays well. And if I might add, it's been rather satisfying. Chicago Herald subscriptions took a leap up. I never thought . . ."

"You stupid bitch. If you wanna play, do it somewhere else. There's a lot at stake here."

"Look, if the fire is too hot, get out of the kitchen. And don't you ever call me a stupid bitch again. Do you know how useful it will be to have Helen Wells for a client? Of all people? Think about it. Look ahead a little."

"All right, but next time let me know." Click.

Chapter 9

"OVER HERE !" HELEN was already contemplating into her first drink.

"There you are."

"Oh, I'm sorry."

"It's alright. Want to talk ?"

"They're the same, Harry. I don't know how I would manage without you. Am I . . . I've been at the bar for ten minutes, waiting for you."

"I should have been more specific."

"I get woried whenever you need to talk to me as opposed to me being a burden on you? Tell me, Harry, am I?"

"No, but if you take a breath between sentences, you'll think better."

"I'm thought out. Between the studio and the column and this." She flicked a white envelope already on the table toward Harry. There was no return address and it was badly worn. Harry was already guessing at the contents, assuming threat or blackmail.

"What is it?"

"Before you read it, you must promise me to never . . . never . . . tell· anyone. No matter what happens. This is the most I've ever asked you, and I've asked a lot, I know. Can you do that?"

"I've managed so far."

"This is different. Do think about it."

"Can you imagine me saying 'No'?"

"Harry, it's from the President."

"The President of what?"

"The President."

"Oh, God." Harry looked down as if the envelope was a revealing clue. "Harry, I need your help." Helen started to cry. "I don't know what to do. I just . . . need your advice . . . That's all . . . Tell me what you . . ."

Harry stroked her hair with his right hand while pulling the envelope toward him with the left. "I promise." He then opened the envelope while Helen occasionally looked up to watch.

"This isn't so bad," Harry lied. "He just needs someone to talk to—that's all. It gets awfully lonely up there. Especially when you've had a spat with your very own Congress."

"Harry. Please . . . There's no return address."

"Maybe he forgot. He's awfully busy, you know."

"Harry, don't patronize me. This is serious."

"When you gain your composure, I'll stop patronizing you. I wanna see TOUGH."

"OK. I'm sorry. See? . . . Eyes are dry . . . Smile . . . The epitamy of tough . . . All right chou guysh. Now will you be serious?"

"Yes, anything to stop that bad act." Harry looked at the letter again and rubbed his chin. This alone soothed Helen somewhat.

"Know what I think? You don't really know what he wants. Only that he considers you courageous and wants to communicate with you. Quite a compliment, if you ask me. So, don't be so upset. Do what he asked you and see what happens."

"What if it's not him. Maybe someone else wrote it."

"It's embossed with his seal."

"So?"

"I have an idea," Harry said and proposed an excellent plan of insurance.

"OK. You're right. What is it about you? I feel . . . well . . . not so scared anymore. At least not panicky."

"When did you get it?" Harry waived the letter.

"Two weeks ago."

"No wonder you've been such an insufferable crab."

"Was I really?"

Harry just wiggled his eyebrows, then began to laugh.

"What is it?" Helen was picking up on the laughter before knowing it's reason.

"Do you realize you may be the first reporter with the Prez as an inside source?"

"Hey, that's right," Helen squealed and then both drifted to the future. Their faces slowly became serious like soft silicone returning to its original shape.

*   *   *

The list of appointees was completed. Nathan appreciated the importance of having good people in the area offices. He felt a real committment to run a fair region with minimum fraud. Only he still had no instructions on how the program was to be administered. All he could do is set up the best machinery, staffed by people who would implement his guidelines in a compassionate manner. After all, the CEA was meant to help people get more out of life. But he had seen a good thought turn into a callous system before. Not in Region Five. Not with self starters like Fred Parks in Lansing and Alice Trevon in Milwaukee. He would have his secretary type up the appointment notices first thing in the morning. He was grateful he did not have to go through normal Civil Service channels for these positions. In a week, he would have to meet with them. To tell them what? To work dilligently at their assigned responsibilities—whatever they were. Nine o'clock struck on the pendulum IBM before Nathan remembered himself.

He realized what he really wanted was a quiet, no-conflict dinner with Helen. He wondered what Helen wanted. He was doing his best. He had not strayed from his values. What more can a man do? He wanted to show her. His region would not become a red tape nightmare. It would serve people. That was his committment. All of his life, he had watched the bureaucracy compound the very problems it was created to solve. Self serving activities. Justifying its actions by its existence. Creating the very needs it serves to perpetuate itself. Never admitting fault.

Just forging on to some invisible purpose. Incapable of virtue and compassion. He could understand why Helen had a disdain for

112

government agencies. Many irritated him too. But they were not all bad. He already knew many good people who were caught up in some system. But they were good, honest, hard working, dedicated. They just were not high enough in the organization to really change anything. Now he was. He could demonstrate how to cut through the bureaucratic machinery. He was not just being naive and idealistic. It could be done, Nathan insisted to himself. The people in his region would get their rights without delay. And the rip-offs would be discovered. He would not just live in his office—not aware of what was happening out there.Helen would see. Someday, she might even write an article on how Region Five was different, he fantasized. Or maybe even do a special.

CHAPTER 10

JOHANNA BAUMBERGER HAD adapted to America. She would tell her new aquaintances that she was going through her second childhood. Since her second day in the U.S., she kept her right cheek bandaged. If her skin became inflamed, she would wear a scarf. No one beside Ingrid and Josef had seen her disfigurement. After a while, Johanna realized that no one was staring at her as she always assumed. No one knew how ghastly it looked. For her age, she still had an excellent figure. Ingrid accompanied her to several fashionable shops and helped select a wardrobe, undergarments, shoes and even the famous pantihose. Johanna had given up on ever attracting a lover and would settle for friends. She did enjoy the stares that came her way. They were different. No pity or embarrassment or avoidance but genuine interest. Perhaps even lust. She had her hair cut short; went on a diet—sort of. Sometimes men would pass her going in the same direction and look back.

In the following week, Johanna was to move to Chicago with a friend from her short childhood. A widow. Her friend had a small clothing shop. Business was good and Johanna would be a good sales lady. "They'll love your accent," her friend told her. It was all very exciting. There was nothing in Bavaria for her. She never could find good work. She felt old and ugly then. But now, it was all so wonderful. Every Mark she would repay to Ingrid and Josef. With interest. She learned about interest from a new charge account. Johanna read constantly when she was not going for walks. In a few days, she had her American History examination.

Then she could become a citizen. She hoped the questions would not be too difficult.

*   *   *

On April fifteenth and sixteenth, the President attended a mayors' conference. Eleven troubled cities were represented. Requests and demands for funds was the predictable topic. Every word was carefully weighed. The proposals were endless and taxing. Scavengers with starched politeness. They would have scratched his eyes out if it would have helped them. The President's mind wandered frequently. It was five thirty and no sign of relent. He considered one more item, agreed to study it and reconnnended a dinner break. All agreed swiftly since it meant more time and opportunity later.

The President rose, mimicked by the others, and left for his room. He asked his Press Secretary to join him. The Secret Service men remained outside and in the adjoining rooms. At five fifty-eight, he turned the television on and found WRX-TV. Then he waited. His secretary could see the tension but had no information to respond with. Helen delivered her news program as usual with one minor exception. The President now had an ally.

*   *   *

In order to minimize costs, the CRA contracted the joint services of the Departments of Treasury and Defense to accomplish the mammoth task of issuing every American over sixteen years of age an ATTRACTIVENESS RATING FACTOR. The IRS was best equipped to handle the announcement mailings. The Department of Defense provided its medical facilities in conjunction with the draft board facilities across the country.

Few areas were really prepared for the resulting response. Metropolitan areas had to resort to appointments immediately. Not long after opening the doors, the appeal requests started streaming in. Mostly those with high ARF's protested, but occasionally, someone would demand a higher rating. There was little levity after the first month. Interested participants soon translated the lower ratings into significantly higher dollar benefits. The fund was open ended. The Cosmetic Equality Agency wanted to avoid pronouncing a limit to the total number allowed in any one ARF category. The code engineers concentrated on language for a fair, objective set of rating criteria. Never the less, there were as many interpretations of criteria as there were participants.

Helen did her best to point out potential inequities in her column. She was accused of giving people ideas to confound the system. Helen countered by accusing the CEA of implying people were stupid (and ugly).

The reactions of the first months of CEA programs were mixed. Helen received many supportive letters for both her news commentary and her column which was by then openly attacking the CEA. However, the rate of voluntary participation in obtaining ARF designations also remained high.

Helen wrote an article titled: <u>The Irony of It</u>. She pointed out the origin of the Act. A woman felt she was denied a potential for income, for dollars, based on the way she looked. Now the Government has not only made financial reward based on looks legal, it has made the process an institution. Helen transfered most of her anti-CEA energy to the column. In case of trouble, it would be easier to replace than the anchor woman position.

The prework package for the ARF examination arrived several weeks after Helen sent in her request card. The package consisted of a questionnaire, exam center listings and a description of what to expect. She decided to drive up to Racine, Wisconsin where no appointment was necessary and she, hopefully, would not be recognized. The actual examination was unnoteworthy. Helen spent five minutes without clothing. There were two female raters who behaved quite professionally.

Still, it felt odd for her to stand nude and turn about purely for observation. Somewhat like auditioning for an exotic dancer's job. Helen wondered what they really looked for and what her rating would be. How humiliating this must be for some, she wondered. And how many raters across the country would misuse their power of judgement. She tried to engage the raters in a discussion on criteria but was curtly informed that talking was not allowed. Perhaps Nathan would be willing to discuss rating criteria—under different circumstances, of course. Similar circumstances, however, turned out to be an enjoyable fantasy.

With little delay, Helen received a new Social Wellbeing card with her ARF number included. She proudly displayed her number nine. Her immediate reaction was to feel a tinge of remorse at not being a ten. That feeling was the origin for Helen's next column. She demonstrated that while the CEA was designed to achieve cosmetic equality, in actuality it formalized inequality. If a nine feels bad for not being a ten, how must some people feel after the Government tells them they are, for example, a four when their boyfriends were treating them like an eight.

*   *   *

The chatter over beer, coffee, cocktails or milk was about ARF's. No place could one go without someone soliciting a reaction to the ARF concept. This would usually be followed by a subtle request for a person's ARF. It replaced the Zodiac for cheap banter. Social stratification was inevitable. As homogeneous layers in a heterogenous liquid. For a time, money, character and breeding slipped in snob criteria. London commentary was particularly witty in assessing the democratic nature of ARF's and their effect on the mating habits of North American sapiens.

*   *   *

In an effort to maintain a link of communication, Nancy McGee asked Helen to stop by the agency. Helen complied and received a suggestion to change the column's name from Helen's Comments.

It lacked energy, Nancy offered. A more suitable heading might be Take Another Look. North approved the change and threw in some advertising to re-educate the fans on the new title. The novelty of a new heading weighed little. Helen still felt restless.

Nancy used an engaging word in their meeting, 'Energy'. Helen had more of it to give than there were receptacles to absorb. The air of caution around WRX was obvious and justifiable. Broadcast licenses were changing hands more frequently. All caution justified, there was still the problem of frustration. "Harry, I have an idea!"

"Right . . ."

CHAPTER 11

THE REQUEST FOR ammendments to the Act were so numerous that regular monthly hearings were announced through the Federal Register. Cities of regional offices were the customary sites. The first such ammendment to make it all the way through the machine was one to eliminate the ARF rating of zero. Proponents, whose organized assemblage called itself WE'RE NUMBER ONE, submitted that rating of zero was demeaning. People with such acute cosmetic deficiencies had problems enough without further degradation.

The ammendment brought Helen's reaction into print. The article, 'What's Your Number, Baby' maintained that the ammendment was a clear demonstration of admitting the sociological impact of ARFs. By assigning actual numbers to the results of nature, zero or ten, an undue concern, comparison and competition of natural inequity was generated. Even without revealing one's number, people perceived each other more in terms of numbers than ever before. Previous to the era of ARFs, a delightful personality could better compensate for an unattractive appearance. ARFs contributed to decreasing the importance of all non-cosmetic factors in interpersonal relationships.

* * *

From one of her customers, Johanna Baumberger found out about the wonderful Cosmetic Equality Act. As soon as her naturalization papers came through, she would be able to get one of those ratings. Who knows, she hoped, perhaps something could be done. America had already fulfilled her dreams so far. One more dream would make it perfect. This one she dreamt since she was fifteen. She was very pretty then so the doctors allowed her an anasthetic. Others were not so lucky.

She recalled their screams; her own terror. She remembered feeling the vibration of a scapel cutting through the flesh. And then the feeling of cool air on her teeth, even though her mouth remained closed. Only the threat of death to her mother made her submit to the mutilation. The pain was surprisingly low when the anasthetic wore off. After a few days, she finally looked into a sliver of a mirror nailed up by the barracks. Her first gaze removed what little color she had left. She felt queezy until she looked away. The women in her barracks stared as if her deformity was the worst. It was not.

That was all so long ago. The bitterness finally wore off. For a while, it was transferred to those who made her feel most uncomfortable. But, there was no purpose. So many others died or were in pain or shriveled up with a body described by neither life nor death. So long ago. It felt more like the scenario of a film; watching herself but never having been a part of it. Almost like Johanna was born with a gaping hole in her cheek. It would be odd to have it repaired. It was so much a part of her life after all these years, she was not sure she could cope with the change. At any rate, it was an exciting thought. And it was free.

*   *   *

The National Institute for Cosmetic Health was kept quite busy sifting through the initial set of product and service eligibility applications. Dr. Wheaton was the final authority for any NICH approval. These came sparingly. He would review the degree to which important criteria were met and choose only those he felt were the most suitable. An occasional charge of arbitrariness was ducked by emphasising the importance of quality before the tax payers' funds were put to work. The PUW Secretary found that position easy and popular to defend when called upon to do so.

*   *   *

Helen received a second letter from the President. It was quite short. He wrote that he had reasons to believe an illegal lobbying effort gave the CEA its life and the clout it had. Helen was not to write to him because there was no practical method without interception. He did not want her overtly involved. He would send his aide to contact her in the next few weeks. Meanwhile she was to gather what she knew that might put some light on extralegal/democratic processes. Harry was spared this communication which no longer seemed as awsome to Helen as when it started.

CHAPTER 12

T HE SOCIAL DIVIDING line with ARF's was seven. Below seven, the ratee was generally concerned with benefits. From four to seven usually meant free cosmetics and paraphanalia. Below four, the primary concern was for free surgical intervention. Seven and higher had relatively few financial advantages so in that range, the ARF's were more a badge of prestige.

San Francisco was the first to capitalize when they formed the SEVENUPP CLUB. For those concerned with the good life, membership was absolutely essential. Soon other cities picked up on the idea.

FAIR'S FAIR voiced some interesting complaints about the Club's operations and growth. Their argument was based on the crudeness of capitalizing on the misfortunes of nature, unfair categorization and discrimination. Helen pounced on the contents with a tongue-in-cheeker titled <u>You Made Your Bed</u>. Many of her column articles, as this one, were no more than a series of questions whose proper progression would cajole a conclusion. For example, she asked: Who wanted to categorically quantify cosmetic appearance? If those numbers were FAIR enough to dispense tax revenues, why were they not FAIR enough to classify club membership? After all, FAIR'S FAIR, is it not?

That literary event incited Nathan to break the silence. "Miss Wells, please?"
"This is Miss Wells. Can I help you?"
"Hi. This is Nathan."

"I know. Can I help you, Mr. Tyler?"

"Is the distance that great?"

"You started it."

"OK. Let's s tart over . . . Good Morning."

"Good morning. And how are you?"

"Inflamed about your column."

"But Nathan. It hasn't even gotten personal . . . yet."

"It might as well. What kind of logic causes you to equate this club membership with dispensing benefits to those who have a real need?"

"Well, young man . . ." Helen was two months older and delighted in that accident. ". . . if you take a closer look, you'll see I made no statements. I only asked some questions that confuse me. Perhaps you have some answers?"

"Yes, I do. The difference is discrimination. Or do you uphold denying people their rights?"

"You're talking like a lawyer. It's the law that says when discrimination is OK and when not. It says it's OK to force us to pay disproportionately to some because of an accident of birth. Then it forces us to not discriminate in the people I might want to associate with in a club. Tell me what justifies the difference—the inconsistency?"

"Need—that's what."

"Need? That reminds me. I need your car tonight."

"My car?"

"I need your car. I have to drive to Milwaukee and mine is on the fritz."

"I . . . can't. I'm due at a function in Kankakee."

"But Nathan," you dummy, "I NEED your car. Now, how about it. What's more important, Milwaukee or Kankakee?"

"That's not a need. You can get there some other way. And I'm sure the world will go on if you don't make it."

"Gee, you're right . . . Makes me wonder though."

"What?"

"What did we do before CEA?"

"God, you're frustrating."

"That's me. Frustrating Helen. Guess how many people write to tell me how frustrated I am and all I need is a good lay since I'm obviously just looking for attention." If words could be recalled like defective automobiles, Helen would have.

"I've never heard you talk like that."

"It's not me talking. It's the letters. I never talk that way. I'm above that sort of thing. I don't have any needs. How about you, Nathan?"

"Some days you're too much for me."

"That is probably one of the most honest statements you have made to me."

"Guess it's time to go, huh?"

"With what you must be paid per hour to perform, I suppose you better. Taxpayers want their money's worth."

"What did I do to offend you?"

"Oh, it's nothing, really. Let me tell you something, though. My spies tell me that you are a remarkable person doing a remarkable job. Well, I predict the more remarkably effective you are in serving the greedy vultures, the higher they'll hang your ass before this is over. And that's not from a letter but from me to you. Because I do care. Think about that, Nathan, as you embark on this strange venture. And now it really is time to go. My work has to be competitive."

"OK . . . Bye."

Sometimes, Nathan did know when to shut up. Helen returned the phone with some perceptible unsteadiness, tight muscles and a flush of warmth behind her ears. That would have to go on the back burner for now, she thought. It was time to prepare for the President's emmissary.

*   *   *

A brief interview of the PUW Undersecretary on Public Radio indicated some apprehension on the handling of CEA ammendment requests. He said this was to be a system by the people and for the people but certain limits would have to be honored in order to keep it a quality system; one that could be administered properly and with a reasonable application of funds.

*   *   *

"Hello. Helen?"

"Yes. How are you doing up there?"

"Good. It's an absolute madhouse."

"Of course. Everyone feels more essential that way."

"Oh, I know. I even get caught up in it."

"Careful. Say what prompted Masteson to give that blurb on ammendments on WKPR?"

"Because apparently, we are being flooded with amendment requests. Some have a lot of backing and would make the original Act look like a conservative law."

"Like?"

"Like an ammendment to regulate—are you ready for this—the amount of time different ARF people spend together . . . Hello, are you still there?"

"Yes, I'm sorry . . . Ahm, where did it come from?"

"They haven't told us. In fact, what I told you is hush hush."

"I imagine so. Do you have any written documents on this?"

"That's all I have, a one-page proposal summary with a cover letter."

"Are you still OK with helping me?"

"I'm helping me, remember?"

"OK. Good. Is it all right to call like this?"

"Sure. Just don't use your name if someone else answers."

"I won't. Can you send me a copy?"

"Yup. Say, do you have an ARF yet?"

"Yes."

"Me too. Do you want to know what mine is?"

"No."

"Good. Then I'll tell you. It's a six."

"Have you gotten any free goodies yet?"

"Nope. But I've applied. To not use it with my low rating would make me suspect in my ideological committment."

"I knew you were good for this work. Oh, one more thing. Do you have anything on Nancy McGee?"

"I'll give it some thought. Why?"

"Starting to do a bit of research. Also, would you have anything like an updated Approved Products and Services List and maybe an old one of the same thing?"

"I'll check and send it along with the letter. Better go. The same guy has walked by my office three times now, looking in."

"Maybe he likes you."

"An ARF of six. Come now."

"Soon everyone will be ten and everyone will be so happy, right."

"Yuck! Bye."

"Bye."

CHAPTER 13

WRX WAS ABOUT to dip another toe into the precarious waters of public (and Government) opinion. Helen's request was approved. The authorities involved delighted in the idea of a Man-on-the-Street feature. It would place at least some of the responsibility of opinions on those interviewed. Such a sharing of responsibility may go far to keep WRX out of trouble, reasoned Harper. The editing would have to be done carefully, maintaining a healthy balance of pros and cons. Numerical representation was not as important to the board—just a healthy display of ideas. The details of their expectations were outlined in a corporate guideline letter to Helen.

Harry delivered the letter without the fanfare she might have expected. Instead, there was the restraint of reluctance as he handed her the board's response. She felt uneasy but quickly moved on to visualize the possibilities. To project the earthy logic of common people would offer a host of new ideas. At least there would be some compliment to the daily testimony of experts.

"Why don't you like it, Harry? You appeared quite positive when I first mentioned it."

"You didn't just mention it. You overwhelmed me with it. My response must have been sympathetic resonance to your exuberance . . . I've thought about it since . . . It spells trouble. Ah, ah, I can see by your eyes, you're ready to pounce on me. I'm not disapproving. I'm just a bit scared for you. For us. Things are moving so fast.

Maybe it's my age. I fear the momentum of the free press is looking more sluggish by the day. And if we push too hard, someone will push back."

"I'm sorry. I agree with your fears. As of today, I think fear may be mild—fear reminds me of a sharp feeling like the cut of a knife. This I feel is more evenly distributed. A sick feeling . . . Harry, I just found out they are toying with the idea of controlling, or at least monitoring, the amount of time different rated ARF's spend together."

"That's absurd."

"It's sick, Harry. Sick!"

"Where did you get this from?"

"No disrespect, but my sources have to stay absolutely confidential because they're taking quite a risk. In a day or so, I'll show you a smuggled proposal. You know what—I think it's time to invite a congressman for a friendly chat. Somebody riding the fence, I think."

"Sounds good if you can get someone to commit themselves to anything beside the ambiguous written word."

"When do any of them turn down a chance to blow their horns?"

"Lately, horn blowing looks down five points. They're waiting to see where the market goes."

"There is bound to be someone who isn't planning on running again and who wants to be able to relate to his kids when they grow up."

"Try, my dear. Try. I'm sure you'll have the viewers and Seegraph's support."

"Hey, it would be a great way to kick off the Man-on-the-Street feature."

*   *   *

The MCGEE IMAGE, founded by Ms. Nancy McGee, formerly of Rucker, Snells & McGee Associates, announced the opening of offices in New York and Los Angeles. This according to a two column ad on the third page of the Wall Street Journal.

*   *   *

"Nathan, please?"

"Just a moment, please. Mr. Tyler is in conference."

"He just finished. Tell him Miz Davis is on the line—from FAIR."

"Well, I'll try but I'm certain he can't leave his conference."

"Helen, what's up? This with reluctant courtesy."

"You medlers. You know, ever since two or more were gathered together in the name of public good, some heavy has been ripping off the populace with taxes. After a while, it became like acne. We learned to live with it. But when you damn meddlers even dare to discuss controlling the amount of time different ARF ARF's spend together, you've got a battle on your hands."

"It's only a proposal. How did YOU find out?"

"Nathan, I could tell you what brand underwear you are wearing today. And your tacky secretary. By the way, is her coffee as good as mine?"

"Jesus, we had a tight lid on that. How in the hell . . ."

"I've got people all over the place. Nice thing about bureaucracy is that the bigger and meddling it gets, the more loose ends there are. Probably our best guarantee of some freedom. I have one source that would blow your mind. In Washington, of course. I'm going to watch every move you make. Sometimes you'll find out what Masteson is going to do next from my colmnn before you get his twix. Sometimes I know before Masteson knows what he's going to do next. What do you think of that? Maybe PUW should step aside and let FBI do the work so mine could be declared illegal. You can tell your boss the people will hear it first in the Windy City. In your district, Nathan. They'll ask you if you can't somehow . . . control that uppity broad. What will you do then? Put a contract out on me? Life is cheap. If you don't mind lack of finesse, you can have me put away for fifty bucks. They'll promote you to the assistant of the assistant of the Undersecretary. But if you don't have me put away, I'm just going to keep screaming. I could find you a job in the mail room. Want me to send you an application?"

"Jesus, you'll ruin me. Will you hold off a couple of days? It's only a proposal."

"Why, so you can have time to make it a law? Nathan, it's like my daddy always said: 'In government, promulgation follows proposal or denial as surely as feces follows food'."

"What happened to the refined, quiet, classy lady I once knew and admired?"

"She's pissed, Nathan. Very pissed. But not at you, my dear Nathan. Your heart isn't black enough. She's only disappointed in you. You could change all that. You could take a stab at being a man. You know this proposal is the most macabre nightmare the Government has considered since it vowed to eliminate poverty. Fight it, Nathan. Make me proud. Or I'll fight you. You'll get a sample tomorrow night. And then my column. It'll hurt, but remember: It's only the beginning. This will be the last time I leave your name out of it. But your boss will be upset. He'll ask you to do something with me. Better get ready for that one. What you gonna do, huh Nat?"

"Jesus . . . What? . . . Yea, I'll be right there."

"I've got to run now. Kisses, Nathan."

"Jesus . . ."

Helen assumed he hung up sometime that day. A copy of the proposal arrived as promised. Helen vibrated with adrenalin as she read the paper. Because of its summary format, it appeared more curt than expected. No justification. No embellishments.

RESTRICTED: REGIONAL DIRECTORS, AREA DIRECTORS PROPOSAL 8749-333-05CEA IN THE INTEREST OF ACHIEVING THE INTENT OF THE COSMETIC EQUALITY ACT, IT HAS BEEN VIGOROUSLY PROPOSED THAT IN ADDITION TO DISPENSING BENEFITS WEIGHED BY COSMETIC APPEARANCE, WE IMPLEMENT AN AFFIRMATIVE ACTION PROGRAM TO INSURE PEOPLE WITH LOWER ATTRACTIVENESS RATING FACTORS HAVE REAL OPPORTUNITY TO EXPERIENCE THE BENEFITS INTENDED BY THE COSMETIC EQUALITY ACT.

IT IS PROPOSED THAT THE SOCIAL ASSOCIATION OF VARIOUSLY RATED, UNMARRIED CITIZENS BE ENGINEERED

TO ACHIEVE A BALANCE BETWEEN THOSE OF HIGH ARF'S AND LOW ARF'S. SPECIFICALLY, THE FOLLOWNG TIME WEIGHTED FORMULA WOULD APPLY:

$$AF = (T_1ARF_1 + T_2ARF_2 + \ldots + T_nARF_n) / 5T_{total}$$

WHERE AF = ASSOCIATION FACTOR

T = TIME IN HOURS OR FRACTION THEREOF

ARF = ATTRACTIVENESS RATING FACTOR OF EACH INDIVIDUAL OF ASSOCIATION PER ELIGIBILITY CRITERIA

TO ALLOW FOR NATURAL FLEXIBILITY, AN INDIVIDUAL'S AF, AVERAGED OVER A MONTH, WOULD BE REGULATED TO THE RANGE OF FOUR (4) TO SIX (6). IF AN AF OF SIX IS EXCEEDED, THAT INDIVIDUAL WOULD BE IN VIOLATION. IF AF REMAINS UNDER FOUR, THAT INDIVIDUAL WOULD BE ELIGIBLE FOR COMPENSATION. EACH INDIVIDUAL FALLING IN THE CONTROL CRITERIA WOULD BE REQUIRED TO FILE A MONTHLY AF FORM AND SUBMIT TO AN ARF RATING IF NOT ALREADY DONE.

PLEASE CONSIDER THE DESIRABILITY AND FEASIBILITY OF THIS PROPOSAL. IT IS OBVIOUS AT THIS POINT OF THE CEA PROGRAM, THAT MANY PEOPLE STILL DO AND WILL SUFFER FROM DISCRIMINATION BASED ON ATTRACTIVENESS, EVEN AFTER MAKING FULL USE OF LEGITIMATE BENEFITS PROVIDED BY THE CEA.

DISTRIBUTION OF THIS DOCUMENT MUST CONFORM TO TOP SECRET PROCEDURES.

JACOB E. MASTESON, PHD
UNDERSECRETARY, PUW

During the editorial portion of her program, Helen had the AF formula displayed behind her while she made several projections on the implications of implementation. In her column, she simply printed the proposal, verbatim, adding only that this was intercepted and not intended for the sensitive eyes of the unwashed masses—yet. These bits of communication did cause a stir. Not enough, however, to deter the inevitable course. Although lacking in degree of impact compared to the proposal, Helen scrutinized the APPROVED PRODUCTS AND SERVICES LIST for some tell tale patterns. On a hunch, she visited Rucker and Snells Associates. The meeting was very congenial and lacking in substance. Neither gentleman was willing to disclose the identity of their clients or any habits of Ms. McGee. The crucial question—if Ms. McGee took any significant clients with her—brought a cautious exchange of glances with a motion to end the inevitably fruitless meeting. It was not a neon sign but sufficient.

Catherine Products had a major portion of the approved products on the list. From what Helen knew of cosmetics, there was no reason why at least three other major cosmetic industries would not have a more significant share of approvals. It was relatively simple to ascertain the advertising firm for Catherine Products. Beyond that link, the doors were closed.

CHAPTER 14

ONE EVENING, WHEN Helen stopped to buy gasoline, a car pulled up from the other direction. She realized she was blocked in at the self service pump. She felt awkward sitting there motionless. The driver of the other car did the same. After some elongated minutes, the attendant reminded Helen of the self service money saving feature of his station. Helen batted her eyelashes, pulled back her shoulders and, with a hint of stress, proceeded to manipulate the attendant to pump fuel and unwittingly provide protection. Her opponent remained motionless and, with silvered glasses, covered his intentions. When the proprietor left, the opponent made his move. Helen froze and left her window open. When the opponent came within five feet, she regained the presence of mind to start her car, put it in reverse and prepare to leave. The man from the other car had gotten out, lept forward and shouted:

"Helen" just in time for her to disengage her foot.

"What do you want? Who are you?"

"I'm Fred Ricklund and am here to represent the President."

He certified his claim with an official looking identification card. "How flattering. And what would such a deity want from me?"

"Ah, yes. Well. I suppose you have to be cautious. Would you join me in the cafe across the street?"

"No . . . Let's go to . . . someplace dark . . . the Playboy Club."

"Well. All right. See you there. I'll follow you."

"Something different."

They proceeded per agreement.

"How did you know I had a key for this place?"

"I just knew you were a man of the world."

"Oh."

Drinks were ordered and seats claimed. The only table available was an electronic tennis game. It was understood they would play a round. It was close but Ricklund beat her. This was license to continue the feigned hostility. Helen started the next match, "Say, how do I know you're legit?"

"How do I know you are?"

"Your problem. Besides, I've already been inspected and stamped. Where is your stamp?"

"I.D. not good enough, huh?"

"Who prints more counterfeit money and information than your little company?"

"OK. I'm impressed with your caution. Now let's get on with the work. What do you need to check me out to your satisfaction?"

"Didn't the President give you something?"

"No. For your protection. He said you would know what to do?"

Helen softened a bit: "Tell me what method the President used to check me out?"

He did. They exchanged what information there was and Ricklund left.

A large gap still existed between the relationship of Nancy McGee and the House Speaker. And the link between the two was only a hunch. It was, however, the President's hunch. Ricklund said they were in the process of checking through party contributions for the year prior to the CEA proposal date. For Helen's next special, she decided to just interview one person and eliminate some of the perhaps justified criticism of trying to cover too much in a half hour. A senator from Montana had decided to resign. The Printing Office friend inadvertantly discovered this when a new name was added to a Senate Armed Services Committee mailing. When she called to double check the correctness, the secretary said he was replacing Senator Latten when he quits. Helen acquired Senator Latten's agreement to appear for interview.

During the taping, some time was spent in reviewing Latten's most important accomplishments while in office.

He appeared calm. The camera did not have access to his perpetually moving foot under the coffee table.

After the midprogram commercial break, Helen asked, "Senator, why are you resigning your Senate seat? So far, you've refused to explain to anyone."

"Pure anger, Miss Wells. Pure anger . . . ," He now moved the fingers in his right hand in sympathy with his left foot." . . . We're a proud people in Montana. I'm sure there are proud people left in many States. I was elected because my constituents believed that my rational approach to government would best represent their interests.

Well, I'm no longer rational when I sit in the Senate Chambers or in the committee or anytime I'm even in D.C. So, I no longer feel I should represent my people."

"Senator, by your record, you've been a fighter all of your life. Now you plan to stop fighting. Why?"

"Miss Wells, if you know that by walking into an alley, fifty thugs are waiting to beat you to submission and the only relief is to give up not only your wallet but promise to come back with your friends' wallets, not going into the alley is not giving up fighting."

"Are you saying the Senate is made up of a hundred thugs?"

"No. Certainly not. For the most part, they are good men and women. Even those I disagree with. That's what a Senate is for—to settle philosophical disputes by weight of reason. The good men and women are still there. So is the building unless someone has decided to liberate it from its burden. What is no longer there is the weight of reason. It is now the weight of fear. It's like the McCarthy thing in reverse. McCarthy was concerned with those forces intent on giving away the farm as we say back home. Then, of course, it got out of hand. I remember those weird times. But this is even worse. Now the IN thing is to give away the farm. And we have the thought constables keeping close track of all of us. What started as a humane effort to make sure that in the process of progress and commercial competition, we don't trample human dignity, has gone berzerk. Everyone is scared to speak their mind. Just hang on to our seats. And for the priviledge, we pass every damn give away program that comes along. Nobody thinks about the cost, the ultimate effects. The looting. You don't have to think about it, you can see it all around. But everyone is too busy to see. They're all engrossed in taking. And the Congress is just trying to get elected. Look at our President, nothing but a figure head. He was a fighter, too. But he is broken. Congress is a machine with totally predictable output. Doesn't matter what party you belong to. Or what your values are. You either vote yes, yes, yes or soon you don't vote at all. But it's not really the Congress.

Everybody in there has felt the ultimatum. And this is really why I'm resigning. It's the people were representing.

Most of them have been wisked along in Uncle Sam's Great Giveaway. Half of them forgot how to take care of themselves. I used to think the midwest was exempt but it's not. Even the farmers. The Feds have been manipulating the agribusiness so much that by now even the farmer expects to get bailed out hy the Government after every hail storm. I never thought I'd live to see the spirit of the American farmer broken. Now it's just a few scattered individuals who haven't joined the Great Giveaway—other than to pay for it. So, I'm quitting. Not because I don't deserve to represent my people but because too many of them don't deserve me. I'm too much of a man. I haven't stopped fighting, but I'm just not going to walk into that back alley again. I'd be ashamed to represent Montana or any other State under these circumstances. I'd be proud to represent a group of people who don't want to be given anything."

"How will you represent them?"

"I don't know, yet."

"How will they find you?"

"That's their problem. They'll have to look for me before I'll represent them. And even then, I'll have to see what they have to offer. The poorer or weaker or dumber they are, the more they'll have to convince me because they'll get more in return."

"The one sentence I dislike most about my job is, 'Our time is up,' but it is. Senator Latten, would you like to leave an address where you can be reached?"

"Yea. Montana."

"Thank you Senator Latten for talking with us and thank you ladies and gentlemen for watching. I would like to remind you that next week on WRX News, we will be starting our Man-on-the-Street feature. We may even interview some women."

With a wink, she returned to casual conversation with the Senator. During this time, she suddenly thought of her old friend, John, with a sharp nostalgic pain. She felt badly that he still had not made an effort to communicate with her. She wondered if he ever watched her program or read her articles; if he was even in the area. She tried to discern some similarities between him and the Senator. There were some. The comment about the alley is something John might have said. Except John would never have been a Senator in the first place. He was the only man she knew that ignored, as much as possible, any kind of government. He just painted. And sometimes ate. She must write to him soon, Helen decided.

CHAPTER 15

I N ORDER FOR the Amendment to be comprehensive, all citizens from sixteen to sixty-five years old and single were required to attain Attractiveness Rating Factors. Each person in this category was then required to submit monthly a CEA Form 100. This Form requested daily Association Factors and the computed average for the month. Each person was also required to maintain a daily log on CEA Form 101's. These logs were provided in books of thirty-one blanks with a completed sample. They could be obtained at any post office if one was not yet on the CEA mailing list. The CEA would audit returns involved; the honor aspect of this approach was stressed. Along with a schedule of fines. First violation of a fraudulent Form 100 brought a hundred dollar fine. The second, five hundred dollars; then one thousand, then ten thousand and one month in jail; then five thousand dollars and twelve months in jail. If funds for payment of fines were not available, the monetary penalty could be traded for jail sentences at the rate of ten dollars per day. Failure to have a set of Form 101's available for audit started at the five hundred dollar level. Since the filing of forms would require only a few minutes a day, no serious problems were expected. Forms could be mailed or deposited directly in mail boxes without stamps. An annual summary Form 102 had to be submitted on April fifteenth each year. The Form could be attached to the income tax return.

An income tax incentive program was also provided. For every tenth of a point below an annual Association Factor average of four, tax payers were allowed to reduce their final income tax due by one percent. Conversely, for everyone tenth of a point above an AF average of six, the tax payer owed an additional ten percent. For annual AF's of over eight, mandatory jail sentences would also be imposed.

Popular support for CEA hit its first major plateau. Resistance was not so much against their approach on principle as it was against the many loopholes. Not only were there more requests for amendments but also amendments to the amendments.

Dr. Wheaton, NICH Director, was compelled to allow the approval of indirect cosmetic services such as encounter therapy, health farms and several quasi-religious groups that offered tangible self-improvement services. Certain criteria would still have to be met.

Two amendments to the AF Amendment were readily approved by the National Advisory Committee of Cosmetic Equality. Congress accepted the NACCE recomendations. The first of these amendments came from the Chief of the Joint Chiefs of Staff who demonstrated that the armed services could not possibly be constrained by the AF Amendment and be expected to function effectively and within budget. The second amendment was more interesting. Proponents maintained that the AF Amendment, in its present form, still did not satisfy the CEA's intent. Since a graduated income tax is used to better redistribute income, they suggested it seemed logical to graduate the AF formula. The equation was thus ultimately amended to:

$$AF = (ARF_p (T1ARF1 + T2ARF2 + \ldots + TnARFn) / 5T_{total}$$
where ARF_p = Personal Attractiveness Rating Factor

The WE'RE NUMBER ONE organization lobbied for a factor of $(ARF_p)^2$, but this was rejected by the NACCE as being too complicated since too few people surveyed knew algebra. The selling point of the formula, which found its way into the latest informational brochures, was: Not only does this latest amendment more fairly distribute association times but for those with an ARF of less than five, it provides additional income tax benefits in those cases where high ARF citizens are not in plentiful supply. It also demonstrates the continued openmindedness of the Government in attempting to achieve equality.

* * *

"Excuse me sir. I'm from WRX-TV and would like to ask your response to the Cosmetic Equality Act as it now stands."

"Sure, whatchya want?" This was a rugged man, late fifties, coveralls, who had exited just then from a hardware store.

"What is your livelyhood, sir?"

"I raise hogs, some chicken. Do a little welding on the side. That's why I'm here. Ran outa rod."

"Tell me, do you currently maintain a Form 101 for the CEA?"

"What the hell fer? I'm just around hogs all day anyway, heh, heh, heh. Hogs, get it. Ha, ha, ha."

"Ahm, do you submit a Form 100?"

"Nope. Ain't intend'n to neither."

"Do you file income tax?"

"Sure do. Got ten bucks back last year."

"Aren't you concerned with being fined or arrested for not filing with the CEA?"

"Do I look cuncerned?"

"You certainly don't. What will you do if they come to arrest you?"

"Arrest me? . . . I'll kindly asks 'em to get offen my prop'ty and if'n they don't, I'll have ta use my shotgun. Can't just come walk'n on a fellers prop'ty when I ain't done noth'n to nobody."

"Thank you, sir . . . We've been filming you from over here. Would you agree to sign this release to allow us to use our conversation on television? Otherwise, we will destroy the tape."

The farmer jerked around to confirm the camera. "Well, I suspect I'm talking for my neighbors too, and the missus'll get a bang out of it so . . . so go ahead." He borrowed Helen's pen and signed by the "X".

"Thank you very much." This was Helen's first feature interview.

* * *

Nancy McGee opened offices in Washington, D.C., Olympia, Washington, Austin, Texas and Nashville, Tennessee.

*　　*　　*

Dr. Wheaton distributed a memorandum listing certain cosmetic deficiencies which should be given special attention. For the applicants in these categories, he wanted his staff to review the application questionnaires. Those meeting the criteria would be offered additional benefits if they agreed to go, at Government expense, to the Walter Reed Memorial Hospital. This action was taken to satisfy requirements of Section 2(b) (3) of the Act. Simultaneous to that memo, Dr. Wheaton instructed his staff on one particular phenomenon which, if an application presented itself, he wanted to personally review.

*　　*　　*

Nathan opened a personal—confidential letter: NOW IS THE TIME FOR ALL GOOD MEN TO COME TO THE AID OF THEIR COUNTRY. This was repeated twenty-five times followed by Signed H.

A Chicago based homosexual coalition was appealing to Nathan's office to recommend an amendment to eliminate the built-in sexual prejudice of the Amendment. To only require tracking of association between opposite sexes, they maintained, clearly discriminated against those citizen's choosing to keep most of their associations within the same sex. Nathan was torn between the soundness of the coalition's logic and some predictable results. Since the requests—and approvals—for amendments seemed endless, it was only a matter of time before Association Factor control would spillover into the business community. Nathan had always believed that there was a right answer to any problem. It was always simply a matter of searching deep enough for facts to tilt the scale one way or the other. This time, the deeper he looked, the more impossible seemed a proper resolution of the alleged sexual inequity. Helen's occasional attacks were still aimed at his office even though she used his name. Perhaps, Nathan considered, it was time to raise the white flag for a day. Helen agreed to dinner on two conditions: The restaurant would be a popular, well lit establishment. And, she could mention in her column, with his permission, the jist of the paradox he was so intent to discuss. To her surprise, it was agreed and the white flag was raised.

At the conclusion of the truce conference, Helen insisted on taking a taxi home to afford Nathan maximum time to think while the subject was still fresh. Helen, too, had time to think, and wondered why she was alone. When she arrived home, a letter from Fred Ricklund, the President's messenger, was among her mail. Ricklund was due in two weeks on Friday at a small airport in the Chicago suburban area. He provided instructions on time and location and only mentioned that the purpose of his visit was somewhat of a breakthrough. He had the names of some banks he wanted her to check out. She would receive them in the mail in a few days.

Chapter 16

T HE RATE OF marriages increased to the point of concern and comment. It was obvious that many of the younger couples and others were driven to marriage to avoid the AF requirements and paperwork. What was not so obvious was the number of those marriages which were intended to be nothing but formalities. Many such marrieds never even bothered to live together.

With so many loosely contrived marriages, the divorce rate went up to sixty-five percent. The National Federation of Churches took the first stand against the state of affairs. The AF system was clearly breaking down the institution of marriage, the Federation claimed. As long as marriage was allowed to be a haven for AF cheaters, the continued errosion of one of the most socially stabilizing institutions was predictable.

The amendment machinery was temporarily with no substantial amendment to consider. Therefore, a study of impact on social institutions was ordered on recommendations of the Cosmetic Equality Review Commission. Their input suggested that in order to prevent further impact on the institution of marriage, the time spent between spouses should be held exempt. The Commission also provided a caution on possible impact on business lest such associations might fall under reporting requirements.

Helen was amazed at such a casual mention of business impact. Even an amateur consideration would reveal a significant upset to any part of commerce or production which involved two or more people. With a mandatory quota of thirty percent women stratified at all practical levels of an enterprise, everything from assembly lines to committee meetings would require some juggling. About half way through a similar discourse in her own column, Helen again scooped the wire services. From her talk with Nathan, she was able to make a reference to the question of homosexual inequality. From this particular writing, she deduced that it must have been required reading for the Washington CEA'ers because the day after her reference appeared in the Chicago Herald, Masteson publicly denied any consideration of homosexual AF requirements. The denial backfired with yet another discrimination outcry. The homosexual protest was well organized nationally and probably waiting for the opportune catalyst.

In response, the NACCE formulated a comprehensive package that was to break all prejudicial barriers. The seed of this project was known to Helen, and she begged the business connnunity to stop being so passive. Since the Government waived the requirements for inflation impact studies on all matters concerning CEA, Helen recommended to the National Hall of Commerce that they make their own effort to attach a dollar figure to this latest scheme. Quite the opposite happened. Even the small, independent firms wained in opposition activity.

Once, Helen caught the owner of a print shop for her renamed Human-on-the-Street spot. He reluctantly admitted that fear of inspection reprisal kept him very quiet.

*   *   *

Alice was not calling Helen as frequently. The conversations they did have were strained. The flow of information ceased. Alice's last call was to tell Helen she would be out for four weeks. Alice decided to use her two weeks vacation after her two week stay in the Hospital for cosmetic constructive surgery. Helen stopped asking questions but remained cordial.

*   *   *

Fred Ricklund's letter arrived on the same day that Helen felt like having a boondoggle. Three banks were named in Fred's memo. One was located in Park Ridge, one downtown and a third one in Joilet. Helen headed for Joilet but thought even that one was closer than what Nancy McGee would have used for a cover account. The MCGEE IMAGE business card had Nancy's photo on it. Assuming she looked about the same one year ago, Helen showed the card to all the tellers. Helen hoped for a younger lecher. She got a middle-aged lecher. Unfortunately, he turned out to be more defensive then lecherous. His bank's honor had a very high premium. This was the direction she pursued: "Mr. Doyle, I'm investigating a political payoff of tremendous magnitude. If you do not volunteer some useful information, it should be obvious that you and your bank may be charged as co-conspirators."

"You're just a reporter. I'm not obligated to give you anything. What makes you think you can just walk in here and threaten me?"

"Sir, that was not a threat. It was simply a statement of a highly probable coming event. Where you place yourself in the probable future is totally up to you. The best you can do for me is save me some time. The best you can do for yourself is to save your integrity. Are we finished yet?"

It worked well. Not only did Doyle provide what Helen needed in documentation, he stated most pertinent facts from recall. Obviously, this small suburban bank had not had too many one million two hundred thousand dollar depositors. After such a lucrative discovery, Helen was impatient for Fred's visit.

Friday, Helen left about an hour before Fred Ricklund's intended arrival. As she approached the airport, she noticed a great many cars parked along side the road. She entered the waiting area, confirmed that the flight was expected on time and took a seat. Helen barely had time to get comfortable and get some chewing gum when she heard a crash followed by a tremor that shook the windows. Immediately sirens sounded nearby. A vague announcement interrupted the background music. It requested that everyone ignore their human nature. Visibly upset, Helen left the airport alternating between general fear and paranoia. She zig-zagged her way through some back roads to the proximity of the crash site. The only advantage was a better view of the smoke. She was stopped by two uniformed policemen with a further supply in the waiting. The men were pleasant, so she chatted for a few minutes to avoid thinking. The policemen seemed to know little more than Helen. As their insulted pride worked its way to the surface, they volunteered that their instructions were to permit absolutely no entry. They were authorized to fire upon anyone who violated their command. What appeared peculiar to them was that over fifty FBI officers were immediately at the crash site and took full charge of the scene. One of the policemen added that he got a call from another local deputy who claimed they prevented the crash rescue equipment from coming closer than a hundred feet, supposedly for their own safety. The equipment was not used.

Helen thanked the men and drove off feeling more apprehensive. She did not know much about how crashes were normally handled but agreed on the peculiarity of the FBI presence. The voice from the car radio further elaborated on the incident: "Twelve passengers and a crew of four were reported dead. The aircraft, except for the tail section, was left fairly intact. The deaths were attributed to burns and asphixiation. Since the impact location was about a half mile short of the runway, the rescue equipment was delayed beyond effectiveness. The area was immediately cordoned off by local police. It is requested that sightseers not attempt to go near the area in the event of secondary explosions.

CHAPTER 17

THE NACCE RECOMMENDED that NICH work with the Social Wellbeing Administration to devise a method of simplifying some of the AF paperwork. The filing requirements were the first significant sources of public objection and would have to be improved with some alleviation.

Helen waited for someone from the President to contact her. Nothing came. Her Government Printing Office friend reported that business was good in D.C. A lot of condolences were expressed on the death of Fred Ricklund in various official documents. For the first time, Helen asked her how she personally felt about the CEA. She said, "I pretend like D.C. doesn't exist. I pretend like my job doesn't exist and sometimes I even pretend I don't exist. I'm sure an ample supply of grass is the only thing between me and arson." Helen was glad to have such a friend but was quite concerned about her.

Helen never mentioned to anyone her presence at the airport Fred Ricklund was destined for. Nor the conversation with the policemen. Then one evening, she found a note slipped under her apartment door. The message asked her to come to the Union Station and said it was urgent and related to the crash. He would recognize her if she showed up about eleven that night. There was no way her curiosity would allow her to ignore the request. There was no way her fear would let her pursue it comfortably. She would be done with the news program by then and could make it by eleven fifteen. Helen called Harry and told him that she had to meet someone for some information but that she was frightened. She asked him to not interfere but just wanted him to know. Harry had fallen asleep when she called and was still wrestling words and logic when she hung up.

As Helen walked down the steps from the north entrance to the Union Station, a young man moved from a phone booth and approached her. They shook hands, surrounded by new train arrivals, and chose one of the many waiting benches to sit and talk. His name was Charly Nunn. He was about twenty-eight and portrayed a curious mixture of refined manners with a potentially crude, almost aggressive use of words.

"Miss Wells, I'm an undercover man for a Federal Circuit Judge in Chicago. I belong to a six-man fencing ring which is linked to a national operation we're trying to close down. I'm taking a hell of a chance talking to you, but I had to do it."

"What do you do? I mean, how do you know about the crash and my interest in it?"

"I'm a thief on probation . . ." He waited for a reaction but only got attentiveness. ". . . I decided I didn't want to spend the next ten years locked up but enjoy stealing so much that I sort of switched sides. Anyway, we were going to rip off the plane that crashed. We did rip off the plane. Christ, you should have seen the guards. In the middle of the goddamn night, men standing in the middle of nowhere in suits. Jesus, was I scared. I didn't know what kind of hardware they had. We don't carry any iron, of course . . ."

"Of course."

". . . Right. Anyway, I happened to get a suitcase that belonged to one Frederick M. Ricklund."

Helen turned pale, and Charlie noticed. "I'm sorry. Was he a friend of yours?"

"Well, not really. Just an acquaintance, but I'm sorry he was killed. We were working on a project of his."

"I'll say you were. There was a manila envelope that had a lot of details."

"Oh, my God." Her eyes said the same.

"It's OK, Lady. I'm with you. I watch your program when I can, and I read your column. The Judge I work for is with you too. He obviously hates rip offs. I can't tell you his name, but I talked it over with him, and he told me what to do."

"Which is?"

"To get the hell out of town for three months and mail you this package."

"Were any copies made?"

"No. I didn't even read it all. The Judge didn't see it either but has a general idea. This McGee chick must be quite an operator."

"Apparently so, but then you know more than I."

"I suppose so. Anyway, what I wanted to tell you which is why I didn't mail this is what else the Judge told me. Don't know how he found out, but one of the passengers was an FBI operative. He sat near the galley. All the passengers and crew except the FBI guy and the co-pilot died of cyanide poisoning. What the news failed to report was that they had nine times the lethal dose in their blood. That doesn't sound like death by breathing burning plastic fumes, does it? That's not all. The barometric device that operates the altimeter had a puncture in it. Which is why, probably, they crashed a mile short of the runway. I know about the autopsy, but I don't know how the Judge found out about the altimeter. Anyway, there were fifty-three FBI waiting before the crash, and they were at the site so fast that not a single local cop had access to the immediate area. I've got to split. Keep an ear tuned to the FEC . . . oh, the Flight Examination Committee and see what they cite as the reason for the crash.

The Judge doesn't know I told you about the cyanide and all that shit, so take it easy on me."

"I will. Thank you very much for telling me all this. You'd better go then."

"Right. You're welcome, and I'm really glad I got to meet you. That really freaks me out."

"Thank you. Good night and take care of yourself. Why don't you become a florist ?" She winked and he waived her off.

Helen figured this man was somewhat acting out his fantasies but was probably trustworthy in this matter. She needed a list of the passengers to confirm the reason for this assassination if that was what really happened. It does explain, she thought, the presence of all the men she saw. But if one of their own was on board . . . No, this was all a bit too much for her. Anyway, she decided, it was done and there were bigger catastrophies ahead.

* * *

Johanna Baumberger was sent to a buying exhibition in New York City. She was to represent her shop's European Dimensions. She had demonstrated quite a knack for fashion. Her honest appraisals and recommendations brought a healthy stream of return and new customers to her friend's shop. New York was dazzling for Johanna.

While there, she met a production manager of a clothing manufacturer. His family was from France. What started as a friendly rivalry became a warm friendship. Near the end of the week, it was obvious to her that this gentleman wanted to share more than conversation and repast. All of Johanna's insecurities returned. There was no good reason to refuse because she was very attracted to this man. No reason but fear. He was to call her by six to discuss dinner. When Johanna returned to her room, she found the message light blinking. It was a telegram, forwarded from Chicago to ask her to contact a Dr. Wheaton of NICH. She was to discuss her application for CEA facial surgery. All haste was necessary if an opening the following Tuesday was to be taken advantage of. Johanna made her call and found she had to depart on a one o'clock in the morning flight. She was excited, scared and relieved that she had a good excuse for her gentleman friend without offending him. There was something strange and unsettling to Johanna about Dr. Wheaton's voice. Perhaps, she concluded, it was just the pressure of making such a rapid decision that bothered her.

* * *

Alice's post-operative ARF was eight. She enjoyed walking by shop windows with dark backgrounds. The novelty of her beautiful breasts was slow to wear off. She joined Milwaukee's SEVENUPP Club and found that post-op sevenuppers were snubbed by the originals. Following her superior's transfer, she was promoted to Milwaukee Area Director of CEA. This news came in a letter to Helen. And went unanswered.

* * *

All schools receiving Federal assistance, either directly or through the State Governments, had to demonstrate a program of Cosmetic Equality Affirmitive Action. CEAA as applied to schools meant that the administration was required to document a reasonable effort at giving preferential attention to low ARF students. Student ARF's had to be assigned by a concensus of two teachers per student per the annual class photograph. Since this process was described as somewhat subjective, the Principal had to approve the final ratings and submit a compliance report to the Superintendent of the school district. Compliance with this order was subject to random audit. Schools found in non-compliance would lose all Federal revenue assistance for three years and State assistance for one year.

* * *

Helen discovered the Flight Examination Committee of the FAA pronounced the cause of the Chicago crash as PILOT ERROR after a closed hearing. The Pilots Association appealed for an open hearing but was denied. The Social Wellbeing Administration announced plans to eliminate the social wellbeing tax. It was only a small contribution to the entire fund demands. Along with this change was a new record keeping system to streamline the submission, dissemination and storing of imformation. This would involve a card similar to a credit card. The entire back would be of magnetic tape. The front face would have a photograph of the bearer and the Social Wellbeing number with the ARF number as the tenth and eleventh digits. The magnetic tape would provide a video or log printout of all vital statistics. The announcement went on to list all entries as: Name; Social Well-being Number; Address; Occupation; Employment History; Income History; Bank Accounts with Balances and Account Numbers; Real Estate Holdings and History; Insurance Policies and Numbers; Education

History; Political Persuasion; Military Service with Branch. Rank, Specialty Codes, Clearances, Permanent and Temporary Duty Stations; Organizations or Membership; Physical Condition and History; Organ Donation Agreements; Marital Status and History; Language Facility; Passport Status and Travel History; Professional Certificates; Medical Qualifications; Skill Certificates; Religious Affiliation; Traffic Citations; Criminal Record; Finger Prints; Voice Print; Aurora Print; Financial status and History; Intelligence quotient, Race; National Origin with Five Generation History; Children's' Names, Social Wellbeing Numbers, Custody or Occupation. Also stored in the tape was a color print out capability of the front and side view of the entire body without clothing. adaptable to laser-vision monitors. The full body printout would only be available to authorized CEA Attractiveness Rating Personnel and Inspection and Compliance Officers. Likewise, asset information would only be available to the IRS and financial institutions. Every precaution would be taken to protect the privacy of information. Except upon the issue of a Federal Court Order, no information could be released to any card scanning device without the consent of the card holder. This would be accomplished by the card holder submitting his or her own secret seven digit number. Only after a central computer verified the proper matching of the secret number with the Social Wellbeing number would the printout be available to a card scanner. Scanners would be coded such that only relevant portions of the total store would be scanable. Fraudulent use or input of equipment or information would be punishable by a ten thousand dollar fine or ten years in Federal Prison or both.

To reduce the staggering costs of the Social Wellbeing system, these measures had to be taken. As a result, the PERSONAL CARD could be used as a drivers license, bank card. diploma, passport, credit rating, resume, etcetera. Any business or government office gaining advantage from this system would be taxed or charged accordingly for each printout request. Federal income tax requirements would be reduced by two and a half billion dollars. Filling out millions of forms would be eliminated or reduced both in the private and commercial sector. Many types of fraud would also be eliminated. There was no end to the advantages and effectiveness of this new system.

A thirty-second public service announcement required of all national radio and TV networks, displayed a hyper PR man citing the PERSONAL CARD as a major breakthrough that allowed people to return to a more simple way of life.

*   *   *

Mexico, Europe and Japan offered temporary (and permanent) disfiguration treatments guaranteed to reduce ARF's by a selected number of points. A more amateurish example, cited by Helen, was one couple who blotch-dyed their skins, pasted on various scars and disfigurations; injected Novacane into their mouths to cause drooping, established false residency in separate, nearby communities, were awarded low ARF's, used benefits to attend a health farm together near Scottsdale in Phoenix and purchased a BMW with their combined income tax return. Since Arizona had not satisfied Federal requirements to administer their own State program, the apprehension of this couple was a Federal crime punishable by ten years in a Federal Prison.

The NACCE surpassed its initial reform package when it recommended BISEXUAL ASSOCIATION FACTORING and elimination of marital exemptions. The ammendment was passed in Congress but only after the Senate Committee added a formula adjustment. All martial associations would be weighted, according to this adjustment, by a factor of eighty percent and all business associations by a factor of seventy percent. The resulting formula became:

$$AF = (ARF_p(T_1 ARF_1 + T_2 ARF_2 + \ldots + T_n ARF_n + 0.7\,(_{Tn+1} ARF_{bn+1} + T_{n+2} ARF_{bn+2} + \ldots +\,_{Tn+x} ARF_{bn+x}) + 0.8 T_{n+x+1} ARF_m)) / 5 T_{total}$$

where ARF_b = ARF's of business associations and ARF_m = ARF's of legal spouse

$$T_{total} = T1 + T2 + \ldots + T_n + T_{n+1} + T_{n+2} + \ldots + T_{n+x} + T_{n+x+1}$$

The benefits of a flexible, responsive government were cited with the announcement of this Ammendment.

Contests were promptly voiced by people who claimed that their involuntary associations incurred at their jobs unjustly penalized their social lives. The Committee foresaw this problem and had already engaged in the formulation of a comprehensive Occupational Cosmetic Equality Ammendment to the Act. Business was given a six month abatement period which followed a two month comment period. Hearings for comments, as usual, were held in all major cities. In Chicago, only three businesses were represented in a giant, nearly empty hall at McChormick Place.

Nathan broke his last thread of private allegiance to the CEA. His public support and discharge of duty continued without blemish. He felt he needed Helen more than air.

She was in Washington to visit her friend at the Printing Office, Marcey Brighton. Helen measured Marcey's energy. She confided in her and requested Marcey to become a link to the President. She gave her a letter of introduction and set up an appointment with the President's aide. The rest of the weekend was a warm rejuvenation of their friendship. Their talking and giggling marathon had no more space for the CEA.

CHAPTER 18

A DATA PROCESSING firm came out with an inexpensive registration device that could reasonably be owned and maintained by most firms with high people volume. The device allowed dual registration of two PERSONAL CARDS, thus eliminating the requirement of documenting that portion of association on Form 101. For about the first year, tapes would have to be sent to central processing. After that period, telephone lines could be rented to directly input all registrations to Federal Central Processing.

This device was greeted with popular acceptance. It became an advertising premium for restaurant and entertainment industries. Affluent individuals could also purchase the registration device and lease a telephone line to community processing centers. Larger industries could lease or buy a time card system which had each employee's time weighted monthly Business Association Factor programmed into it. With this advantage, some people would be able to go an entire month without having to make a single Form 101 entry. The CEA approved the waiving of a Form 100 in such instances. Instead, a form 100A could be submitted with nothing but the Social Wellbeing number and the community code on it. Federal Central Processing would do the rest.

*   *   *

The Department of Defense ordered all military personnel to attend a four hour course on Equality Philosophy. All Effectiveness Reports had to include a statement that the officer supports the intent and philosophy of the Cosmetic Equality Act in his or her daily mission.

*   *   *

A man in Twin Falls, Idaho reportedly committed suicide after his PERSONAL CARD information storage at Federal Central Processing in Baltimore, Maryland was unable to be corrected for three consecutive months. He was unable to withdraw funds from his bank, drive his vehicle, gain access to public buildings or even prove his identity. His survivors are temporarily denied all government benefits until the identity problem is corrected.

*   *   *

Alice Trevon was the guest speaker at the National FAIR Congress.

*   *   *

In the pile of mail and messages waiting for Helen's return from vacation were five messages from Nathan. In increasing order of desperation, Nathan wanted Helen to return his call. She did and was swept off to lunch.

"Where in the hell have you been?"

"On vacation."

"I know. I know. Why didn't you tell me? I was going crazy."

"You were? I couldn't imagine why."

"Where did you go?"

"Hey, what is this?"

"I'm sorry. I didn't mean to be nosey. I just . . . well, I mean I only wanted . . . ahm . . . to know . . ."

"If I spent two weeks with a man, right?"

"All right . . . Yes!"

"Nathan, did you ever try just being straight and leave the politician at the office?"

"Well, I thought you might be . . ."

"Offended, Nathan. Come on. Out with the words. Your questions won't offend me. Not asking them when you want to will. Take a chance, Nathan. If I'm offended then there isn't much between us, is there? It's a great way to find out quickly."

"Hey, leave a little for me, huh."

Neither noticed their shouting or the attention they were drawing from people at surrounding tables.

"Nathan, make a decision. Quick. Courage. Do you have it? Yes or no? Well? Time is flying by. I had five messages to return your call. What could be so . . ."

Nathan reached for Helen's shoulders across the table and kissed her for the first time. When they settled back into their chairs, Helen was stunned and her eyes opened wide. Then she closed and covered them with one hand while she regained her balance with the other. Nathan reached out to meet her. "Woman, I don't understand you. One minute you're a hard ass and then you're a . . ."

"Nathan, shut up for once."

"Ha, ha . . . No, you shut up for once. And I'm starting to understand me. You know, I'm starting to understand you. And that's what I wanted to talk about. With the last amendment, I think I heard industry's spine break. I know what is coming next. Every business with any number of employees will have to hire a full-time Equality Manager or a at least the services of a consultant. Businessmen will have to go to the slums to be with a wino so they'll be permitted to work together in committees and not exceed their AF's. Assembly lines will have to be retooled. Affirmative action programs will try to achieve an ARF equity of five within each plant or business.

Corporate taxes will be adjusted according to AF averages. There will be inspections, fines, appeals. Then there will be more amendments to amend the inequities created by the last batch of amendments. And each week I pick up the Chicago Herald, read your column as it takes another notch out of my pride. As cutting as your comments have been, I see that you've been kind. You've been waiting, haven't you? And I've been an ass. Every night, I watch you on the news. The last two weeks, I didn't even have that. Sometimes, I felt like you were talking to me—looking right at me. The other viewers were just uninvolved bystanders. It was like being a little kid when I'd sit there in church with my parents. The minister would be shouting at my sinful ways and I didn't know what the hell he was talking about but I felt sorry for whatever I did. I was doing my best but he kept right on shouting.

Just like you. Seems like all the things that came natural, he would ask me to deny. Just like you. Except what comes natural now is what that raving man taught me. So, here I am again, being yelled at. This time by a woman."

"'Who's yelling?"

"A sneaky woman who uses newspapers and television just to get at me. All those other silly people think you are doing it for them, but I know it's all aimed at me. But there is a difference. This time, I'm feeling bad. Not because of the shouting intimidation but because I really feel it. Somewhere, deeper in my mind, I really know what we are doing is wrong. But I can't allow that feeling to be recognized and keep my job. Facts are what I've always lived by. And love of humanity. And the desire to help. It comes naturally. Then you come along and ask me to deny it. My feelings are still with all those neople who get so little out of life. But now I am projecting the outcome of our folly. Soon it encompasses all of our other follies. Then I have to ask: Is it all wrong or misguided? Is there an elephant in the middle of the room and everyone pretends it doesn't exist? And the longer we pretend, the more committed are our organizations to continue on the same path. Picking up momentum. If one program is good, two are better. What am I to do with this feeling of reaching out to help people. It can't be wrong, can it? I mean, who wants a world of callous people. Loving each other, helping each other—that has to be good. That's my essence. So, there you are. In the paper; on TV; on billboards even. And, with the energy of ten normal people, you are telling me my essence is wrong. You make fun of my activity. You even make me laugh at it. Isn't that crazy. In fact, the most penetrating things you have ever said or done are the ones where for a moment you would make me laugh at us. At myself. But you weren't really making me laugh. I was laughing because it was a natural response to your train of thought. Why, I mean, how could I laugh at what I've dedicated my life to? It's like spotting a 'Made in Hong Kong' stamp on an old, handed down Spanish heirloom. I'm sure

I've seen the truth peak through before on occasion, but I've learned to ignore it. Isn't that what our parents teach us to do? It was too upsetting. What was different this time? In this political-social chess game, you are supposed to be my opponent. So, who do I yearn for when my empire develops a crack? While you were gone, and I couldn't find out where you went, I was beside myself. I don't know why I went to work. I don't even remember what I did.

I'm shattered. I don't know what to do with tomorrow. Helen, I love you."

"Nathan . . . Nathan . . . Breathe . . . Shut up . . . Not just your mouth but your mind. Give it some room . . . Let go for just one day and see what happens. One day . . . Pretend like you're that kid again. Before he thought about right and wrong but instinctively knew. Before he belonged to a gang. Back when he took his parents' love for granted. Before his minister taught him about sin . . . Are you there yet?"

Nathan was concentrating on the glass of water, wearing a slight smile. Helen remained silent for another minute and said, "Now, what do you feel? What do you want?"

Never having gone through this progression without previous planning, Nathan was surprised to hear himself saying, without a waiver of nervousness, "I want you."

"Wow."

A happy waitress found herself with a twenty dollar bill to cover a $9.75 tab.

* * *

The CEA Director was himself surprised that the AF system had not yet been challenged in the Supreme Court. In fact, the current challenge was from a computer firm which had devised a system of rating that was more objective than any human could be. It would also eliminate the disagreeable (to most) process of disrobing in front of a panel of raters. The company, Scanning Processors, Inc., had their machine advertised in both scientific and popular magazines before even approaching Dr. Masteson's office. Dr. Masteson already had received several inquiries from Congressmen on the 'Scanner', but dismissed their importance.

He saw it as a skillful advertising ploy that would mature in time. With increasing CEA opponents making waves on the separation of state and industry, he wanted no part of suggesting facility or equipment improvements.

The demand came. Masteson's patience paid off. He called for a demonstration for himself, his advisory staff and all regional directors. Nathan watched and listened with disbelief. A nude subject stepped into the scanning booth. An apparently gentle set of guide bars made contact with the shoulders, hips and mid thighs to assure the subject was properly positioned. Various printed instructions lit up throughout the process which lasted about two and a half minutes. The same was repeated with a female subject. A printout was made available from each sequence. It broke down the final rating into one hundred subfactors. A copy was reproduced for each attendee. The sales representative then explained each subfactor and the weight given to each in relation to the overall score. Everyone was astonished at the number of things that could be considered in the attractiveness of a person. Even functions such as sight, hearing, voice pattern and body odor were included. What intrigued the staff the most was the method of measuring the shape and size of the penis. One member voiced the question of the possibility of measuring the penis while distended since that could be an important attractiveness factor. The representative explained that it was considered but eliminated because it might be offensive to human integrity and the time of the scanning then could not be held constant since stimulation time could vary too much. Everyone felt magnanimous by agreeing to give up that bit of information.

The ARF scanner demonstration made a positive impression on almost everyone. The device soon was in demand and money was made available. Nathan gave Helen a synopsis of the scanner and its purpose. She never mentioned it in her work. Helen finally felt a strong urge to write to her artist friend, John. She also stopped feeling guilty about not having written earlier. It had been a year and a half since they last communicated. All she had was an address for Honolulu. When completed, it was a nine page letter about a man she loved, his journey to facing reality, the horrid art displays and, most lengthy, her frustration with her work. It provided sustenance and sanity for some but she complained of having no real impact. The more clever her attacks, the more dishonest was their reaction.

*   *   *

Helen's friend, Marcey finally met with the President. It lasted less than a minute and occurred in one of the shopping aisles of the commissary. The meeting was long enough to establish a channel of communication, linking him again to Helen Wells. Nothing else was discussed. When Marcey related this event to Helen, however, she matched it with an even more significant event. She found out that a special study case for advanced cosmetic surgery created a bit of upheaval at the Walter Reed Hospital. When Dr. Wheaton arrived to interview a Miss Johanna Baumberger, she apparently went berzerk. The event remains a well kept secret, and Miss Baumberger remains at the hospital under sedation, not necessarily at her request. Apparently, the minute she saw Dr. Wheaton, she jumped out of bed and clawed at his face with both hands. All the while, she was screaming things mostly in German, but the word Nazi was discernible. Marcey asked Helen not to make the incident public because the source may be traceable. She promised she would check into it further to see what it all meant.

CHAPTER 19

NATHAN STARTED TO show up late for work, take long lunches and entire afternoons off without explanation. Sometimes, he would sit all day with a carafe of wine, waiting for Helen's dinner break. She knew what he was going through and never mentioned it once. He would have to deal with his new awareness in his own way.

After some weeks of ignoring his state of mind, Nathan felt like discussing his turmoil. "Now I know how a prostitute feels," he started.

"Oh, do you now? And how is that?" She was extremely cautious and continued her sarcastic format.

"To do something for pay when you don't believe in it."

"Are you sure that's what prostitutes feel?"

"Well, I've never been one . . . that way."

"I think we've all been one. A prostitute is simply a person who receives material gain for using her body to satisfy someone else's needs without her personal, emotional comrnittment to anything but technique. She—or he—may very much believe in what they are doing. Now tell me what is the difference between that and what millions of people do everyday when they go off to work? Or to bed with their legal spouse as your formula calls them?"

"Well, there is a difference with your job. It's not sexual."

"You mean they use a different part of their body, right? What if they just used their hands, like an assembly line worker?"

"Then it depends on what they did with their hands. I mean it matters whether it's personal."

"Then where would you put a waitress that is pleasant and smiles prettily for a better tip even though she's having her period, her feet are killing her, she just had a fight with the cook and has a pounding headache? And her customer is a jerk."

"What are you trying to say?"

"That you are a mental prostitute and that's even worse than the most degrading slut I can conceive of because her mind might still be resolute but she's hungry. Before you get angry, my love, let me confess that I am too."

"You? You're patronizing! If there is anything I know about you it is that you are not a mental prostitute."

"You are wrong."

"Then explain. You have me all confused."

"No, you're not confused. My facts are different than yours but only in degree."

"You mean I'm a bigger prostitute?"

"I don't know. Depends how you look at it, so it doesn't really matter. The fact is that I have kept quiet when told to. I've gauged the acceptability of my columns and, most importantly, I continue to pay my taxes."

"Taxes even. God, you're dragging everything into this."

"Look how much of my income goes to support all the crap they have deemed mandatory that I totally disagree with but continue to pay for. It's no different than being a secretary by day and screwing for money at night. It still comes down to one third of my working time in something I'm not committed to. Oh, I'm more subtle than a prostitute. Kind of like a housewife that screws out of duty to keep the meal ticket content. Except, I suspect the meal ticket knows the difference between screwing for money or security and making love. My bosses know when I've compromised my nature—even when they haven't dictated it. The important thing is that the public thinks I'm incorruptible. And that is what they think, so I'm a marvelous success, right?"

"I never would have . . . wow . . . I don't know what to say."

"Cherish those moments. They are rare and pure in honesty. Don't say anything. What do you feel?"

"Sorrow . . . fear . . . love for you."

"Isn't that enough?"

"Right now, it's great. But tomorrow, I have to go to work again. And that is . . . ugly."

"Nathan, you know I haven't interfered with your life, your decisions. I haven't wanted to and still don't. They have to be yours. But, I can't pretend to be other than what I am either. Look at your last statement. Every word of it. And you might find your answer—if you're ready."

"Which statement?"

"About work."

"Oh . . . Tomorrow . . . I . . . have . . . to go to . . . work. It's 'have' isn't it?"

"Is it?"

"Damn you. Yes! . . . I don't really have to."

"Then if you go, it's because you chose to. There is no job in the free world, unless you've been sentenced to hard labor, where there is a gun to your head. Ultimately you go to work because you want to. So accept the responsibility for your decision."

"I haven't decided. I might play hookey," Nathan winked.

"Cop out."

"Hard ass. Give me some leeway."

"It's not for me to give. So, what are you going to do?"

"Wait 'til tomorrow morning and see what I feel like."

"Beautiful. You're getting the hang of it."

"I am, huh? What about you, teacher?"

"Not fair, I'm not used to being picked at."

"Such a bitch."

"We're all the same inside—remember?"

Helen had hired a detective agency with her own money. Harry always saw to it that she was reimbursed. The owner of the agency was an old college friend of Helen's. He always saw his mission in life in being as sneaky and double crossing as his government. While they had many disagreements in those days, she knew what motivated him. He was an incurable anarchist and thoroughly enjoyed foiling any system devised by man. He never was aware how he violated his own principles. When she first met him again, six years after they both received their Degrees, he complained of 'shit' work but seemed to enjoy being at the helm of his successful organization. She did not ask how he got there but accepted him as an old friend. He resisted the term 'old' but soon realized that their relationship and alliance would be a practical and philosophical one with the extras included.

He was wonderfully competent. The last assignment was no exception. Within two months of Ricklund's death, he had used janitorial personnel to discover the nature of most of McGEE IMAGE postal transactions in all her national offices. The contract period was up. The Pergutory Agency forwarded its findings. Every time Helen saw his letterhead, she wondered how many clients he must have lost before he ever got them with such a company name. He did not seem to be starving and had less wrinkles than she did, so it all must have been satisfactory.

The report of the McGee assignment was quite revealing. It appeared from Nancy McGee's mail, that eighty percent of her business was related to products or services approved by the National Institute of Cosmetic Health. Pergutory certainly earned their fee. Since she had so little discretionary time of her own, she decided to also get a quote for finding out the extra-U.S. history of Dr. Wheaton. For five hundred dollars down, Pergutory would activate their Munich agent to discover what could be discovered. The arrogance of his wording always appealed to Helen, and she gladly wrote the check.

*   *   *

An American Archbishop declared that having a monthly AF average of over seven was a venial sin. It was a Catholic's duty to share their God given beauty with those not so abundantly blessed.

The National Federation of Churches. representing most protestant faiths except Mormon and Baptist were not to be outdone. Their best theologians gathered to formulate a unanimous statement on the relevance of AF's and ARF's in the Christian faith. The outcome was that from the latest research, it was obvious that Christ, a physically beautiful person, had an approximate ARF of nine relative to the culture in which he lived. By his choice, however, he associated generally with people having ARF's of about five or less. The apostles probably ranged from one to six with an average of 3.5. This, of course, took into consideration those factors culturally important at that time. Christ's association with the poor and sick, including the leppers, brought him to an average Association Factor of three. By studying the Gospels, it could easily be concluded that Christ put a great deal of emphasis in maintaining a low AF, although, of course, no formal tracking system existed back then. Consequently, those choosing to follow the way of Christ are obligated to pursue a low AF average. This, however, must be done not with the intent of achieving an AF of three but to give vent to the natural Christian compassion for the lowest of men without being aware of one's charity or income tax advantage.

Although the statement, in its entirety, received enthusiastic support, some claimed it hinted at civil disobedience. A follow-up statement made it clear that the Federation did not in any way advocate civil disobedience or not filing Form 100's but simply gave guidelines for the manner in which Christians should relate to those computations. In fact, their support of the intent of CEA was demonstrated by the advocacy of achieving an AF of three. In concluding, the statement cited Christ's example of the coin with Ceasar's image on it.

Since there was much talk of taxing Church property to achieve true separation of Church and State, the Pope declared that artificial birth control was proper in the eyes of God when practiced by people with an ARF of seven or higher in the United States. Low ARF Catholics protested and claimed it should have been the other way around.

The Jewish organizations avoided the subject. When pressed, they insisted they had no interest in any system that rated people but were not opposed to the Cosmetic Equality Act either.

A Buddhist monk in San Fransisco made a public statement that Gautama the Buddha was probably a five, blended in perfectly with the common man, but would never have cultivated the awareness of a personal ARF.

*   *   *

Marcey communicated to the President the known fact of Nancy McGee's business operations.

*   *   *

Nathan woke up on a Wednesday morning before his alarm went off. He looked calm but felt excited; smiled while dressing; saw himself in the mirror and winked. He arrived at his office a half hour late as usual. He asked his secretary to summon the Assistant Regional Director immediately to his office.

"Ralph," he said as nervous Ralph took a seat like an apprehended school boy, "I quit. It's been awkward working with you because I think—no, correct that—I know we're all full of shit. Please have my personal effects forwarded to my last known address. You'd better pick an assistant immediately so you can do the same thing, when you're ready, without causing delay in our great work. You may tell Dr. Masteson, when your voice returns to you, that a written resignation statement will be forthcoming. I want it neatly typed because now it's only illegibly scribbled on twelve sheets of . . ." Nathan covered his mouth and whispered loudly, ". . . toilet paper. Which, incidentally, is where I made my decision. My body taught me something about elimination, and thus I have just eliminated the CEA. Have a really good day, Ralph. I'll flush my own door." Ralph formed the letter's on his lips which were to ultimately hiss out the word 'sir'. But he never got that far. His eyes, however, remained agile and followed Nathan's every move—from his desk, out the door.

The first thing Nathan did after leaving the Federal Building was to withdraw his entire savings from his three accounts, all in cash. He left one dollar in two accounts and twenty-five in the third for a later withdrawal. He stored the cash in a coin deposit locker at Meigs Field.

Then he dropped by Helen's office and handed her an envelope, smiled, kissed her and walked out. That took care of her commentary for that night.

* * *

Purgatory Agency came back with a somewhat predictable, but now confirmed, scoop. Dr. Wheaton, alias Philip Wetter, was a young intern, studying at Heidelberg. Part of his on-the-job training gave him access to a group of prisoners at the Dachau Concentration Camp. Because of his advanced work in the area of skin surgery, specifically the problem of artificial tissue rejection, he had free license to perform his experiments at a Nazi concentration camp near Munich. Wetter's work backfired. About twenty-five victims wound up with mutilated faces, thighs and buttocks. They had the unique aspect of never completely healing. His second problem: He was discovered removing prisoner identification number tattoos from some affluent inmates for sizeable fees. No more information was available, but he apparently was warned in time to escape to England to continue his studies after the war. If more information was required, a new contract would have to be drawn up with the London office.

* * *

The President initiated a prompt reply. He used available resources to try to discover irregularities in the NICH operation but found none. He recommended that somehow Helen try to introduce a product or service so it would wind up on the NICH approved list. This may shed some light on the invisible. Nathan was just looking for a fun project. He decided to create the Synergy Institute, Inc.

Helen received a call from the receptionist describing a man waiting to see her in the lobby. He would not give his name. By the time she arrived down in the lobby, she was totally surprised.

"John!"

"Hi! It's good to see you." They spun each other around.

"You came. I was scared to hope for more than a letter."

"Scared? Why?"

"Didn't know if the address would connect. Or if you would or if you wanted to."

"I've been waiting for a letter from you."

"What are you doing in Chicago?"

"Can't you see I'm visiting you," John teased her.

"Oh, I'm sure. Now why are you really here?"

"Well, I must admit there is a mercenary aspect to this visit. I'm going to open a travel agency here."

"That's different."

John detected a note of disappointment and offered this explanation. "No, I haven't sold out. I just divorced. I divorced myself from Chicago. And I divorced my art from money. We're all trying to be friends again."

"What have you been doing all this time? Wait, let me arrange to leave. I can spare an hour . . . Elsie, will you call Harry and tell him I'll be out for an hour ?"

"Yes ma'am. Where shall I tell him you'll be ?"

"Let them guess."

"I see." This with an impish smile.

"No you don't but that's OK . . . Are you into a walk ?"

"Certainly." John opened the door for Helen.

"Good. First, how long will you be here? Second, can we have dinner tonight? And third, just what have you been doing?"

"Left or right? . . . First, as long as it takes. Second, yes. And third. I've been a tour guide in Hawaii."

"A tour guide? Wow."

"Not just your ordinary tour guide, mind you. I specialize in tours which concentrate on the past and present fine arts of the Hawian culture. Is that lofty or what?"

"I'm impressed."

"Well, it just kind of evolved, but it sure has put bread on my table. In fact, I have a back log of applicants. So, one thing leads to another. A travel agency seems a logical extension. Besides, I can deduct my trips back home."

"That's really interesting. I just would never have expected you to be in the travel business."

"It would be interesting to know what you thought I've been doing."

"I haven't let myself think. I was scared for you."

"Scared for me?""Well, at first I was just annoyed at you for not fighting it out. Then, somehow, I saw you as a projection of me.

Sort of like you are where I might be going. But I didn't want to know where, so I haven't really formed any images."

"What made you finally write?"

"I don't know, really. Just all of a sudden, I wanted to. Quite desperately, actually."

"I think you are right about seeing me as a future projection of you. I hope you're strong enough to take a good look."

"Strong enough . . . Yes, that I don't know. I'm scared right now. I think you might show me what I don't want to see."

"No. Only what you want to see. You have to be ready."

"You sound like . . . Do you actually know something specific that I don't know . . . or see?"

"I've discovered a kind of practical truth . . . out of frustration. I don't know if it will apply to you. Or if you would accept it."

"What is it?"

"I don't know for you. You do or you wouldn't have written . . . I think you're ready to pass through your bottleneck."

They stopped walking for a traffic light. Helen put her head down and thought about how much John had changed; how much stronger his silence had become. Then she asked, "What is a bottleneck?"

"Your fear. Same for everyone."

"Will you help me?"

"No."

Helen was startled. Scared. "Then why are you here?"

"To watch you pass through your bottleneck. To feel the joy of seeing you on the other side. To welcome you when you arrive."

"You sound so confident."

"That's not exactly the right word. I feel a lot of hope."

"What happened to you in Hawaii?"

"Nothing. It happened here. I went there to appreciate it."

"So, something did happen. What?"

"I passed through my bottleneck."

"What was it for you?"

"Like I said, it's the same for everyone."

"How can it be? We've always been in such different worlds. You, the creator—me, the reporter."

"That, too, is the same. My creating reports. Your reporting creates."

"But, our differences. You seemed so accepting of events back then. Almost passive. I always needed to fight."

"No. I fought too. I stopped selling paintings because I refused to sell them at tacky shops. I sat down and said I'll starve if I can't display my work the proper way. It's a different approach but it is still fighting. It's how you relate to it. Passivity can be the most intense form of fighting if you feel the choice."

"Then are you fighting?"

"No."

"Is that the other side of the bottleneck?"

"Yes."

"How do I get there?"

"By not needing to fight."

"It's not something I can control. Why would I want to go through such a bottleneck?"

"I don't 'know."

"I don't know what to say next."

"Good. Remember, I'm not administering a test. It's your bottleneck."

"How do you know I need to pass through it?"

"I don't. What are you feeling?"

"This is weird. That's what I asked my friend before he flipped out."

"Must be a potent question."

"I feel like I'm standing on a ladder, but it's starting to tip and I can't stop it and I can see me falling."

"Do you want to stop it from tipping? Just reach out and grab a branch?"

"For some reason, I don't want to. It would be interfering with what I'm seeing."

"Are you dead when you hit the ground?"

"No, I'm . . . it's blank . . . but I'm not dead;"

"A fighter would grab the branch."

"Are you saying I should stop fighting?"

"Only a fighter says 'should'. I'm not a fighter."

"Sure is hard getting an answer out of you."

"Probably impossible when there is none."

"What if we sat here for two hours and never spoke?"

"It wouldn't matter."

"What if . . . I stopped doing my news casts . . . or my column?" Helen realized that was where her fear originated.

"It would be the same. It wouldn't matter."

"But it matters to me."

"Then you'll keep doing it because that's all that really matters."

"So why do you say it doesn't matter?"

"Because it only matters to you but not to the purpose you're trying to achieve."

"How can you separate me from my purpose. It—what I do—must also matter to those that watch, read or make money from what I do."

"Certainly. This isn't their bottleneck though. It's yours. What's your purpose in your work?"

"It's to . . . report to people what's going on around them."

"Why?"

"Because they need to know."

"Why?"

"So they can make responsible decisions."

"Do they make responsible decisions?"

"Some—a few—I don't know."

"Is art unionized?"

"Yes."

"Why?"

"Because no one stopped it."

John laughed. "Listen to what you just said. Is making babies unionized or collective?"

"No, not yet."

"Why not?"

"Because . . . no one wants to."

"Bet I can find some."

"OK. Not many want to."

"What if many did?"

"I suppose it would be then."

"Could the reporters stop it?"

"Not really."

"Should they?"

"I don't know."

"When would collective baby making go away?"

"When people no longer wanted it."

"Or when there are no longer any people."

"So?"

"When will art go back to art? When will people go back to accepting their appearance?"

"When they're sick of all this."

"Without the reporters' help?"

"I suppose. But reporting may bring an end to it sooner."

"How?"

"By a repeal of the law."

"Won't that make a lot of people unhappy?"

"Make a lot of others happier."

"Six of one, half dozen of the other? So they can regroup and try again? If not with the CEA, with whatever next scheme?"

"Possibly."

"That would mean they didn't learn much."

"Some just don't."

"Who are you trying to teach?"

"Those that . . ."

"What's wrong with the CEA."

"To me . . . it's trying to achieve equality where there is none."

"What's wrong with that?"

"It's opposing nature."

"What are you doing?"

"Trying to . . . stop people from . . . opposing nature."

John smiled at Helen and continued, "What's natural? Isn't it natural in our present society to demand sick legislation? Sick legislation only comes from a sick society. The entire populace is responsible. So, how do you suppose it will get unsick?"

"By educating them on their sickness,"

"Has it had an effect?"

"Not much."

"If anything, education without experiencing the sickness may even slow down or actually prevent recovery.

How many articles and speeches in the last year have foretold the bankruptcy of our treasury. Does anyone care if there is enough money to pay for the services?"

"Apparently not. So what are you saying?"

"If I tell you, you might not really learn what you're trying to learn."

"Then you're not teaching me?"

"I don't care if I teach you. I only care that you understand. Because that's what it will take to get through your bottleneck."

Helen was growing impatient. "You're contradicting yourself. If you were anyone else right now, I'd be angry with you."

"Good."

"Good! Why good?"

"Because you're learning and that's what you seem to want."

"Uch. You're frustrating. What amI learning? That I have a short temper?"

"It's a great start. Listen, I have some things to do. Why don't I head back to the hotel from here? Shall I pick you up at your place or at the studio?"

"At the studio. It will be sooner. So we can finish this conversation."

"It's already finished. I'll pick you up at your apartment at ten thirty. Bye." John looked directly into her eyes, smiled, waved and left.

Helen just stood there and remembered when she was seven and announced she was leaving home and no one turned around to ask why. She realized she had been like a little girl with John. It was like asking her daddy a million questions a long time ago. The afternoon went slowly. While on the air, she made enough mistakes that Harry left his monitor to wander to the news studio. He met Helen on her way out.

"You OK?"

"Yes, Helen snapped, then softened, It' s just one of those days. I think all my biorhythms crossed the line today and got stuck there."

"Your what's?"

"Oh, nothing. An old friend visited today that I haven't seen for nearly two years. It was kind of traumatic you might say."

"That's funny. I thought you were preoccupied with your government friend."

"Ex."

"No more friend?"

"No more government. Definitely a friend. No, this is different. This is my—ah—mentor."

"Oh, I see how it is. And he's menting you quite severely, yes?"

"I don't know what he is doing."

"Well, I hope someone will be interested in mending you after the menting."

"It's supposed to be the same thing, don't you see?"

"Not immediately, I don't. No."

"Get your tongue out of your cheek."

"Get your humor out of your can."

"I suppose so. God, I just feel like everything is closing in on me."

"Quite the opposite. The Universe is expanding."

"Enough. No more smart asses today."

"Same time tomorrow then."

"Get thee hence!"

The taping for the ten o'clock program was quite similar to the earlier one—for which Helen was silently grateful. At its conclusion, she dashed out to her apartment. Such abandonment was against the rules. She decided a shower and fresh clothing were more important.

John came to meet her at ten fifty-five. She knew why and resolved to keep her impatience in check. He showed no sign of faltering confidence. Instead, he was warm, pleasant, and a real gentleman. His tour guiding must also have smoothed some of the rough edges for polite society.

"Hi. Come on in."

"Hello. Thanks . . . It's a very pleasant apartment. I hoped it would be."

"Why?"

"So I could tell you that it was."

Helen giggled. They left and started walking, both assuming the other had a destination in mind. Not until they entered a restaurant and had to admit they had no reservations did they realize this. When they were seated, John broke the silence, "How was your afternoon?"

"You know very well how it was."

"I suppose. Well, you seem very calm now."

"It's a put on. I'm bracing myself."

"For what?"

"For whatever is coming next."

"Did you have something planned?"

"No, not me."

"Well, neither did I. But, I have a great idea if you agree to it."

"Help."

"No, no. Settle down. You even mentioned it this afternoon. So here's your idea but don't agree to it unless you're comfortable with it."

"OK." Helen adjusted herself in preparation.

"Let's eat our dinner and spend, let's say, two hours, here or at least until they throw us out. During that time, let's not say a word, but you continue to think of today's conversation. Every time you feel compelled to ask me a question, just look at me instead and ask the question to yourself."

"For two hours?"

"Too much?"

"Hour and a half."

"It's a deal."

"Can I ask you something first?"

"Sure."

"What are you going to order?" John threw the napkin at her.

The silence began. It was interrupted occasionally in exchanges with the waiter. Helen found it difficult to look up at John at first. When she did, he would be staring at her. Not intensely. Just watching with a very slight smile. Their dinners arrived. A welcome diversion for Helen's mind. And eyes. The plates were empty all too soon and wine was ordered. Forty-five minutes to go. Helen's mind finally wandered to Nathan; what he was up to that night; their recent conversations; their first kiss; Nathan's project—except he seemed to lose sight of its purpose. In fact, as she thought about the two of them, there was suddenly a good bit of similarity apparent between Nathan and John. Two years ago, the comparison would have been absurd.

John was aware that Helen finally forgot about time. Her eyes were focused to someplace behind his right shoulder. With only fifteen minutes to go in a contract both had forgotten, Helen began to smile, still focused on the same point. John thought of reminding her to blink but realized that would have been the grossest violation of the day. Soon, without blinking, Helen's eyes became moist as she looked up at John. Without changing her glance, she stood up, took the seat next to him, embraced him and started sobbing uncontrollably. The waiter came to ask if there was anything he could do but John waived him away before the words shattered the moment.

When Helen was finished, they got up, paid the bill and walked. Although long past their pact of silence, every time she felt drawn to saying thank you, she didn't. John knew the moments from her hand. They never discussed how much he had helped her by refusing to help. They never discussed when they would see each other again or where John would go next. When they arrived at her home, they held each other one more time. Helen cried intensely but without sound. As he turned to go, their hands glided down their arms, past the bare wrists, across warm palms, fingertips, and air. Helen had never been so in love with life.

*   *   *

Turning out eloquent pulp was no mysterious art to Nathan. He soon had an entire package ready for review at the NICH Department of New Products and Services. He used a friend's name, with his permission, as the requesting company officer. A fairly prompt response indicated that the Synergy Institute, Inc. appeared to offer a service that fell within all the guidelines for approval. Formal approval would follow in all likelihood. Meanwhile, an approved advertising agency familiar with government guidelines would have to be selected.

The name and address of the nearest approved agency was enclosed on a data card. The company was, of course, free to select any approved scheme of advertising. To no surprise but still amazement, the data card had the name and address of the McGEE IMAGE office in Chicago.

Upon reporting his find, Helen fully expected Nathan to pop out of the telephone receiver. She would now learn from him how to apply her newly discovered, always known, journey through the bottleneck. Nathan no longer seemed to care about categorizing the good guys from the bad. He was more like a child solving a riddle. She couldn't relate to this puzzle that way yet. But part of her discovery was to allow herself the time she needed to become that child again.

The McGee monopoly was described to the President. Helen and Nathan could not decide if the aftermath was by the President's design or compromise. The McGEE IMAGE offices were shut down without comment. All NICH related advertising contracts went out for proper bid. Nancy McGee was appointed CEA Great Lakes Assistant Regional Director. None of this activity seemed to be very newsworthy. Helen could not muster the energy to change that trend. The puzzle was broken, and they knew who broke it. That was satisfaction enough.

An incident that did make news was Dr. Wheaton's unprovoked attack by a CEA patient. The thrust of the news release was that following some lamentable error during the confusing times of World War II, Dr. Wheaton had dedicated his life to furthering the frontiers of science in the area of cosmetic and reconstructive products and services. Dr.

Masteson proclaimed himself to be proud to have such a dedicated servant of the people in his administration.

Nathan went to the bank in which he had left the twenty-five dollars. He astonished the teller when, as she returned from the readout screen to inform him his account had been attached, he burst out into loud laughter. He left his savings booklet and PERSONAL CARD on the counter and walked out, still laughing. He decided to spend the afternoon on his new sailboat and wait for Helen.

*   *   *

The National Institute of Health announced that the moratorium on recombinant DNA research was lifted to facilitate swifter progress in genetic engineering of cosmetic related chromosomes. The announcement went on to explain that recombinant DNA procedures allow for controlled injection of DNA nucleotide sequences of one organism into the DNA of another. A restriction enzyme severs the double-helix type DNA molecule and permits the joining of compatible foreign DNA segments. After recombination, the new nucleotide sequence made up of cytosine, quanine, adenine and thymine will propagate its new genetic message by normal cell division.

For years, the controversy had been around two feared outcomes of such research. One was the possibility of illegal or hostile use of advanced genetic engineering to create a species of subservient humans. The other was a fear of accidental generation of dangerous new pathogens threatening the human race. The latter fear stemmed from the fact that the only suitable host cell for advanced recombinant technology had been an isolated plasmid from E. coli bacteria which exists in the human intestine. If this bacteria were to be accidentally altered and introduced into the environment, the human race could be destroyed. Proponents of unrestricted research maintained that experimental genetic engineering had created such sensitive strands, that even inadvertent strands could not exist outside the controlled laboratory environment.

With the recent breakthroughs in understanding and controlling genetic mutation errors resulting in dull, highly porous skin, the National Advisory Board for Cosmetic Equality had exerted pressure to eliminate restrictions on the use of E. coli K-12 or its derivatives, as cloning vectors. They also advocated eliminating the requirement for P-4 physical containment level laboratory facilities for purified, characterized DNA research experiments and permitting shotgun type experiments in existing P-4 laboratories.

*   *   *

Marcey sent a rough draft of the Federal Register article to WRX for Helen. Dr. Masteson had just signed an Emergency Temporary Standard requiring ARF adjustment services for all ARF's of eight or higher. The requirements for an Emergency Temporary Standard were met by virtue of parameter indicators that demonstrated the thus far overall ineffectiveness of the Cosmetic Equality Act. The ETS called for immediate designation of candidates for adjustment services. The candidates would be selected at the rate of one hundred per day by a computer with a random algorhythm. All TV stations were required to air the day's candidates printout during the last two minutes of the evening newscasts. For those not viewing television, printouts would be posted daily for public inspection at all U.S. Postal and Telephone Offices.

Helen prepared for the day of the first adjustment candidate printout. A Congressman from Iowa, representing an increasing number of CEA opponents, agreed to a taped interview. The interview was to be aired during the landmark newscast. Nathan asked Helen to consider backing off from her warfare. He did not tell her about the attached savings account. He knew it indicated comprehensive steps to confound CEA opponents.

With only fifteen days between signing and implementing the Emergency Temporary Standard, most people did not really realize the potential impact. Those that did, observed with curiosity. The verbage around the standard was too ambiguous to cause too much alarm.

CHAPTER 20

T HE DAY OF the first printout was accepted with curious apprehension. Only twelve percent of registered citizens were rated with an ARF of eight or greater.

The taping of Congressman Coleman went well. With the emotional appeal of a man involuntarily losing his grip on a child about to drop into a canyon, Coleman described current events. He said many people no longer wanted the CEA. Hardly no one in Congress wanted it anymore. There were no funds to do anything else. The deficit was going out of control while some worthwhile programs were getting vetoed or cancelled. The President vetoed everything that crossed his desk. The country was being run by the major Federal Regulatory Agencies—even outside the control of the President, and they were supposed to be his agencies.

When he finished, Helen asked how this could be reversed. The seasoned Representative, with twenty-eight years in Congress, tears in his eyes and a quivering voice, answered, "I really don't know."

The newscast went well. Helen planned no commentary She asked the engineers to feed the first list of one hundred ARF adjustment eandidates from Federal Central Processing right after Congressman Coleman's tape finished. The list started to scroll down the screen exactly on time.

ARF ADJUSTMENT CANDIDATES COSMETIC EQUALITY
AGENCY RANDOM SELECTION 17 JULY 1986

1. WELLS, HELLEN MARIE
   SW # 9 8 1 2 2 440 7 0 9
2. RADCLIFF, SAMUEL ROBERT
   SW# 7 4 0 3 9 2 8 8 6 0 8
3. SHELL, J . . .

The End

ADDENDUMN

For the past twenty-five years I have been working on a software program for industry to help small companies deal with the infinite requirements of running a business. One of the features of that software—called M7—is that every time you log on a different quote appears at the top of the screen. I find these quotes interesting, witty or inspiring. I don't necessarily agree with them:

- Life is like a roll of toilet paper, the closer to the end you get, the faster it goes. *Anonymous*
- Don't be afraid to go out on a limb. That's where the fruit is. *Arthur Lenehan*
- There is no happier (wo)man than one who lost everything yesterday and got it all back today . . .
- A chief event of life is the day in which we have encountered a mind that startled us. *Ralph Waldo Emerson*
- What lies behind us and what lies before us are small matters compared to what lies within us. *Ralph Waldo Emerson*
- Nothing great was ever achieved without enthusiasm. *Ralph Waldo Emerson*
- It was a high counsel that I once heard given to a young person, 'Always do what you are afraid to do'. *Ralph Waldo Emerson*
- The real struggle is not between East and West, or capitalism and communism, but between education and propaganda. *Martin Buber*

- If you can't be a good example, then you'll just have to be a horrible warning. *Catherine Aird*
- History is the sum total of all the things that could have been avoided. *Konrad Adenauer*
- A celebrity is a person who works hard all his life to become well known, then wears dark glasses to avoid being recognized. *Fred Allen*
- If only God would give me some clear sign! Like making a large deposit in my name at a Swiss bank. *Woody Allen*
- One reason I don't drink is because I wish to know when I am having a good time. *Nancy Astor*
- Outside of the killings, Washington D.C. has one of the lowest crime rates in the country. *Marion Barry*
- We are all born mad. Some remain so. *Samuel Beckett*
- I was court-martialed and sentenced to death in my absence, so I said they could shoot me in my absence. *Brendan Behan*
- It took me 15 years to discover I had no talent for writing, but I couldn't give it up because by that time I was too famous. *Saul Below*
- I don't deserve this award, but I have arthritis—and I don't deserve that either. *Jack Benny*
- We're lost, but we're making good time. *Yogi Berra*
- It gets late early out there. *Yogi Berra*
- I really didn't say everything I said. *Yogi Berra*
- A Canadian is someone who knows how to make love in a canoe. *Pierre Berton*
- We know what happens to people who stay in the middle of the road. They get run over. *Aneurin Bevan*
- To retain respect for laws and sausages, one must not watch them in the making. *Otto von Birsmarck*
- It is difficult to predict, especially the future. *Niels Bohr*
- When you look like your passport photo, it's time to go home. *Erma Bombeck*
- I can't say as ever I was lost, but I was bewildered once for three days. *Daniel Boone*

- The matter does not appear to me now as it appears to have appeared to me then. *Judge George Wilshere*
- There is just one thing I can promise you about the outer-space program: Your tax dollar will go farther. *Wernher von Brown*
- The youth who loves his Alma Mater will always ask not what can she do for me but what can I do for her? *Le Baron Russell Briggs (Kennedy borrowed this line)*
- The tragedy of life is not that man loses but that he almost wins. *Heywood Broun*
- Insanity is doing the same thing over and over again, but expecting different results. *Rita Mae Brown*
- Every day people are staying away from the church and going back to God. *Lenny Bruce*
- I should sooner live in a society governed by the first 2000 names in the Boston telephone directory than by the 2000 faculty members of Harvard University. *William F Buckley, Jr.*
- Sports do not build character. They reveal it. *Heywood Hale Broun*
- Don't believe the world owes you a living; the world owes you nothing—it was here first. *Robert Jones Burdette*
- All that is necessary for the triumph of evil is that good men do nothing. *Edmund Burke*
- Too bad that all the people who know how to run the country are busy driving taxicabs and cutting hair. *George Burns*
- A paranoid is someone who has all the facts. *William S. Burroughs*
- If you think education is expensive—try ignorance. *Derek C. Bock*
- The optimist proclaims that we live in the best of all possible worlds and the pessimist fears that is true. *James Branch Cabell*
- You can get much further with a kind word and a gun than you can with a kind word. *Al Capone*
- There are in England sixty different religions and only one sauce. *Italian Naval commander Francesco Caracciolo*

- Gung ho. Evans F. Carlson (thought this was Chinese for work together but it is actually an abbreviation for Industrial Cooperative Societies)
- The three great elements of modern civilization are Gunpowder, Printing, and the Protestant Religion. *Thomas Carlyle*
- It is better to be vaguely right than precisely wrong. *H. Wildon Carr*
- I shall not die of a cold. I shall die of having lived. *Willa Cather*
- I would much rather have men ask why I have no statue, than why I have one. *Cato the Elder (Roman statesman)*
- The main thing about acting is honesty. If you can fake that, you've got it made. *George Burns*
- The real struggle is not between East and West, or capitalism and communism, but between education and propaganda. *Martin Buber*
- You can observe a lot by watchin'. *Yogi Berra*
- You're enough to try the patience of an oyster. *Lewis Carroll*
- Whom the gods wish to destroy they first call promising. *Cyril Connally*
- Heaven has no rage like love to hatred turned, Nor Hell a fury like a woman scorned. *William Congreve*
- No man is a hero to his valet. *Anne Bigot Cornuel*
- Writing about music is like dancing about architecture. *Elvis Costello*
- One does not sell the earth upon which the people walk. *Crazy Horse (Ta-Sunko-Witko)*
- Tomorrow is our permanent address. *E. E. Cummings*
- Time is what keeps everything from happening at once. *Ray Cummings*
- A man is not old until regrets take the place of dreams. *John Barrymore*
- Take the first step in faith. You don't have to see the whole staircase, just take the first step. *Martin Luther King, Jr.*
- Artists who seek perfection in everything are those who cannot attain it in anything. *Gustave Flaubert*
- Books are not men and yet they stay alive. *Henry Ward Beecher*

- There is no revenge so complete as forgiveness. *Josh Billings*
- Christians are supposed not merely to endure change, nor even to profit by it, but to cause it. *Harry Emerson Fosdick*
- Here is the test to find whether your mission on Earth is finished: If you're alive, it isn't. *Richard Bach*
- If a small thing has the power to make you angry, does that not indicate something about your size? *Sydney J. Harris*
- The real struggle is not between East and West, or capitalism and communism, but between education and propaganda. *Martin Buber (1878-1965)*
- There are only two styles of music—good and bad. B.B. King
- The Russian government is an absolute monarchy tempered by assassination. *Astolphe de Custine*
- The only difference between myself and a madman is that I am not mad. *Salvador Dali*
- I went to a fight last night and a hockey game broke out. *Rodney Dangerfield*
- When I was a boy I was told that anybody could become President. I'm beginning to believe it. *Clarence S. Darrow*
- He has always been stupid. He is just loosing his ability to conceal it. *Robertson Davis*
- If you understand everything I said, you'd be me. *Miles Davis*
- If you don't go to other men's funerals, they wont go to yours. *Clarence Day*
- Treaties, you see, are like girls and roses: They last while they last. *Charles de Gaulle*
- I get my exercise serving as a pallbearer to my friends who take exercise. *Chauncey M. Depew*
- Nostalgia isn't what it used to be. *Peter De Vries*
- Reality is that which when you stop believing in it, it doesn't go away. *Phillip K. Dick*
- One can fool some men, or fool some men in all places and times, but one cannot fool all men in all places and ages. *Denis Diderot 1774 (not Abe Lincoln)*
- Once a woman has forgiven her man, she must not reheat his sins for breakfast. *Marlene Dietrich*

- There are lies, damned lies, and statistics. *Benjamin Disraeli*
- I didn't have time to write a short letter, so I wrote a long one instead. *Mark Twain*
- History rarely repeats itself—but it often rhymes. *Mark Twain*
- As a dog returns to his vomit, so a fool repeats his folly. *Proverbs 26:11*
- The hardest thing in life to learn is which bridge to cross and which to burn. *David Russell*
- He that will not sail until all dangers are over must never put to sea. *Thomas Fuller*
- The tragedy of life is what dies inside a man while he lives. *Albert Schweitzer*
- The most dangerous thing in the world is to leap a chasm in two jumps. *David Lloyd*
- All saints have a past and all sinners have a future. *Anonymous*
- As you have done, it shall be done to you: your deeds shall return on your own head (or what goes around, comes around) *Obadiah 1:15*
- Intellectuals solve problems. Geniuses prevent them. *Albert Einstein*
- You can't fight in here—this is the war room *George C Scott in Dr. Strangelove*

04137562-0091 800